HAVEN

ZONE CYBORGS BOOK 1

JESSICA MARTING

SHADOW PRESS

HAVEN

Haven (Zone Cyborgs #1)

ISBN 978-1-989780-14-5

Cover design by German Creative

CONTENT WARNING:

This book contains discussion of trauma, abuse, drug use and addiction; a supporting character appears under the influence on the page.

For Iris, who patiently listened to me whenever I wouldn't stop talking about setting Beauty and the Beast in space.

CHAPTER 1

THE *GRYPHON* LURCHED SHARPLY PORTSIDE, knocking Cressida from her bolted-down chair. Her hands scrabbled across the top of the wall-mounted desk to keep her small thincomp from crashing to the deck. Its screen was already cracked, its case held together with off-brand Super Seal and she couldn't afford to replace it yet.

What now?

Cressida had hoped that by booking passage on a luxury starship she might not run into the same issues she did traveling with the rest of the masses, but it appeared trouble was determined to follow her no matter what. It was a joke among her coworkers that if a ship or shuttle was going to break down, it would do so with Cressida Merchant aboard.

The intraship speaker mounted above her cabin door crackled, and a man's staticky voice said, "*Gryphon*, this is Captain Tevar speaking. We apologize for the bumpy ride, folks, but we're making an emergency landing at Haven." There was a pause, and he added, "No need for panic, it's just for a short repair that we can't make while we're in the space lanes." Beside the speaker, the wall-mounted clock numbers read 03:10. Hell of a time for anyone to be awake, but Cressida always had trouble sleeping in space.

She perked up at the mention of Haven. The tiny planet just past the edge of Zone space, and was all but abandoned, and off-limits to civilians.

This could be interesting.

The *Gryphon* tilted again, this time to starboard, and Cressida again grabbed the desk to keep from falling over. The captain spoke again. "Please stay in your cabins, and strap in. We're breaking atmosphere in a few minutes. Uh, try to go back to sleep, if you can."

Sleep? Like anyone could sleep with safety straps holding them in place, or during a bumpy planetside landing, even when it was three in the morning. Cressida sat down on the deck-locked chair and raked its safety harness over her torso. The ship's heavy air engines engaged, sending vibrations through the deck and into the marrow of her bones. While the *Gryphon* struggled with Haven's atmosphere, Cressida balanced her comp on her knees and keyed in a search on the planet, thankful the detour hadn't cut off her access to the galactic net.

Haven contains an abandoned former military installation and spaceport ... no known sentient beings ... home to many species of toxic flora and fauna ...

A side trip to the planet sounded sort of fun, Cressida thought, assuming the ship's passengers were allowed to leave. According to the links that popped up, Haven had breathable air and was reported to be full of interesting ruins. She wouldn't mind taking some holos of it all.

She'd heard of the former military installation situated there, stripped down and left to rot less than ten years ago according to the search results. She checked them again. The old base was supposed to be close to the planet's lone spaceport, which was probably where the *Gryphon* was going to land.

Excitement thrummed in her veins. How often did such an opportunity pop up, anyway?

"Absolutely not."

Cressida looked up at the mountain of a man who blocked the ship's passenger entrance and pasted on her best wide-eyed innocent expression. "Sir, I don't see the harm in letting me take a quick peek around off-ship while the crew conducts repairs. I just want to take a couple of holos. I promise I won't touch anything."

"It's not that." The ship attendant's eyebrow arched knowingly.

Damn. Cressida removed a ten-scrip piece from her pocket and pressed it into his hand, hoping that was what the man wanted and not something else. "Will that work for you?"

He quickly opened his palm and took a surreptitious glance at her offering. "It will, for about five minutes outside. And drop the schoolgirl routine. You're too old for that."

Now it was Cressida's turn to raise an eyebrow at him, but he didn't respond.

"Go down three decks to maintenance," the attendant said. "All of the doors down there are open and everyone's working on fixing that fuel line break. If you get caught, this never happened."

A chill slithered down Cressida's spine. "Fuel line break?"

The attendant blanched but quickly recovered. "It's minor. Don't worry about it. This bucket'll be back in the lanes in no time, which is why you have to go belowdecks, stick your head out to get the galaxy's most boring holos, and get your butt back up here before anyone notices."

Even Cressida, with her limited knowledge of piloting beyond personal shuttles, knew that a fuel line break was never minor. On a ship the size of the *Gryphon*—designed to hold up to three hundred passengers, divided into first, second, and third classes—a fuel line break could easily cause a major disaster.

The only consolation she had was that her tiny third class cabin was steps away to the escape pods. "At least we'll be back in Zone space soon," she said.

"We'll only be a couple of hours late," the attendant said. "Now scoot."

Cressida suppressed the urge to roll her eyes at him and tightened her hold on her backpack strap. She slipped into the stairwell beside the lift and made the short trip to the maintenance deck, ducking behind a bulkhead when a pair of overalled techs walked past.

She could smell fresh, unrecycled air as she crept along the corridor, and she turned into the first room she could find. Ah, one of the emergency pod bays. She walked around the tiny two-seater vessels to the huge door yawning open at the other end of the bay, where darkness beckoned. Evidently, it was nighttime on Haven, too.

She leaned over the edge of the ship and looked down. It looked like the escape pod bay was about three meters off the ground, and she could see workers from the *Gryphon* walking around the launch pad the ship was grounded on. Their flashlights bounced off the ship sides and the launch pad, off the overgrown shrubbery and trees that had invaded what was left of the stripped-down spaceport.

Cressida removed her holographer from her backpack. She flicked its power switch and held up the small device, snapping image after image of vegetation colliding with technology. It was too bad she couldn't actually get on the ground and look around outside.

Unless...

She eyed the nearest tree, a massive beast of indeterminate species, but then, dendrology wasn't among her interests. The nearest branch looked strong enough to hold her weight and appeared to be less than a one-meter jump away. She could make it.

She could take some holos, then climb down the tree and hop back on the ship through one of the open doors on the ground, easy-peasy.

Cressida backed up a few steps and took a running leap for the tree branch. Her feet landed on the branch and she vaulted herself forward until her arms surrounded the tree trunk. Her hands landed in sap, and when she moved her feet, she could feel sticky resistance on the soles of her boots.

Ugh.

She looked down and, in the darkness, could discern fanned-out branches beneath her that could function as a ladder. Keeping her hands around the tree trunk, she carefully began to descend, guided by the light spilling from the *Gryphon* and keeping one eye on the ground.

Her feet cleared the ground, and she bit back a grin. It quickly evaporated when she realized just how sticky she was now; the tree sap coated her everywhere. She hoped her thincomp and holographer were okay in her backpack.

Oh, no. She would have to touch her holographer to get those images. *Well, shit.*

Maybe she had some waterless cleanser in her backpack? She wiggled off one sticky strap and lifted the front pocket flap. She touched the small bottle of cleanser and it immediately glued itself to her hand. She tried to take it out, but her hand wasn't cooperating.

What the hell?

A sudden heaviness weighed down her limbs, and she stumbled in the darkness. The lights streaming from the ship faded into nothingness and she moved blindly forward, hoping to catch the attention of one of the *Gryphon*'s workers.

She'd made a terrible mistake.

When she tried to cry out, she found her voice didn't work. Hands waving blindly in front of her, she turned around a few times, trying desperately to orient herself, and crashed into what felt like a pile of overgrown shrubbery. Dimly, she could make out fist-sized red flowers clustered on the bushes. She focused on them as her eyelids grew heavier.

Drowsiness swamped her as soon as she hit the ground, and as much as she tried to fight it, Cressida succumbed to sleep.

An unfamiliar feeling tore through Lukas when the controls of the command tower he called home lit up for the first time in, well, *ever*. He had quickly locked down everything and stayed where he was at the top of the tower. Maybe not the best place in case he needed to escape, but familiar.

Have I finally been tracked down? It had been nearly six years since his escape, but that didn't mean the Zone military wasn't still out there looking for him. In fact, he would be surprised if they weren't. The war was over as far as he knew, but one could never be too sure about wars when it came to the military's Admiral Best.

He had modified some of the systems in the command tower shortly after his arrival to accommodate his personal hardware, changes he was now glad to have made as he pressed his right wrist against a comp panel's input, aligning with the datalink installed there. With his left, he deftly inputted a line of code from memory that would let him access some more information about the intruding ship, with them being none the wiser.

Lines of information scrolled past his vision, and he read every word, scanned every number.

MacQuarrie Galactic ship... passenger starship registered as Gryphon *out of Port Marcel... current captain Harsha Tevar... 297 passengers registered...*

He let out a breath he hadn't realized he was holding. According to his poached information, the *Gryphon* had encountered a fuel line break and had stopped at Haven for an emergency repair.

May the universe bless that ship, because it isn't going to go far with that type of malfunction.

He checked the ship's flight plan and manifest. Ah, it was due to arrive back in Port Marcel in less than twenty hours. The *Gryphon* would make it if they repaired that break.

At least, that's what he hoped. The last thing Lukas needed was for anyone to find out where he was, who he was, and when they connected the dots, why and how he was still alive.

The *Gryphon* had landed in the middle of the Zone nighttime, a schedule Lukas still kept on Haven because he hadn't been able to deactivate his internal chronometer. It was nearly six hundred hours before the ship blasted off, causing violent reverberations through the command tower and undoubtedly terrifying the local wildlife. Or at least what remained of it, Lukas thought ruefully. The Zone's government and military had done a number on this place prior to their abandoning it.

He stayed connected to the comp for the entire time the

Gryphon stayed on the crumbling launch pad, monitoring their communications to ensure no one had an inclination to peek around the old command tower. He conducted a final scan after the ship broke atmosphere, moving images of the launch area running across his vision in a private, albeit boring, vidshow. Beneath it, the comp read the area temperature and offered feedback about environmental conditions in yellow numbers that scrolled along the lower corner of his eye.

They're gone. It was a relief to Lukas, but a bitter one. It was better to be alone on Haven, and free than a product of the Zone's military, built and paid for.

What the hell?

An abnormal reading caught his attention and he froze the stream of information with a thought.

Humanoid female... ident chip F38639.05... body temperature 311 kelvins...

Shock roiled in Lukas's gut for the first time in years, then anger.

He had a stowaway on his planet.

He resumed the information feed while he tried to decide what to do. There were several logical courses of action that would benefit him, and at the top of that list was killing her.

Universe damn it all, I came here so I wouldn't have to kill people.

The sensors reported back to him that she wasn't moving. The only visuals he could pick up were a body lying prone and motionless a couple dozen meters away from the spaceport's launch site. How the hell had she managed to sleep through a starship launch?

Three hundred and eleven kelvins, he noted. That was far too high a temperature for the average humanoid. She was running a fever, and he remembered that the launch area was surrounded by overgrown carnibo trees, a deciduous species replete with toxic sap native to Haven. The Zone militia's chemical weapons division once used that sap to create mild nerve agents.

And she was lying in a double-thorned rose bush, so she was probably scratched all to hell in addition to being poisoned.

"Damn," Lukas said aloud. He finally removed his wrist from its dataport and massaged it with his other hand. A tiny whirr zagged through his arm as the links and chips there realigned themselves.

He was going to have to take a hike to the launch pad, and see what to do with his unexpected visitor, assuming she was still alive by the time he got there.

And along the way, he could decide whether or not he should kill her.

It was less than a two-kilometer trek to the spaceport's launch pad, a trip Lukas rarely made. Why would he? Anything he could possibly need was either inside the command tower or a few meters outside of it, and his needs were minor. The military had made sure of that when he was built.

And he had been built, constructed by the galaxy's finest surgeons and overseen by a Fleet admiral with cool, detached precision. The most expensive weapon the Zone would ever produce. Lukas would never forgive them for that.

Maybe he would get lucky and his stowaway would already be dead by the time he arrived.

No, probably not. Carnibo sap took a long time to work, and she would probably wake up and start hallucinating at some point before she finally expired. Lukas sighed at the prospect. He had to deal with this.

The ever-present readout in the corner of his vision picked

up when he was near the rose bushes, alerting him to her presence. From here, he could see a pair of legs splayed akimbo, clad in black trousers and matching black boots.

She was alive, according to his sensors, and still unconscious.

Lukas moved the rose bush branches out of the way with gloved hands to get a better look at her. A mass of long, tangled dark hair hid her face from his view, and deep red scratches decorated her hands like obscene jewelry. Her red jacket, like her trousers, was shiny with dried carnibo sap, as was the beat-up pack strapped to her back.

Lukas could put his hands on her and electrocute her so quickly she wouldn't feel it.

It would be the most merciful way for her to die.

He bent down to reach for her, but instead of delivering a massive electrical shock he found himself pulling her out of the double-thorned rose bush, rolling her on to her back. The sensors in his gloves fed him information about her high fever, the rates of her respiration and heartbeat, snippets he didn't know much to do with. He wasn't built to be a healer.

More scratches marred her face and neck, including one that stretched across her full bottom lip.

Do it, he urged himself. She wouldn't feel anything, especially since she was already in a deep sleep.

If she woke up and had a way to contact anyone off-world, he was fucked. He could not and would not go back to a life of military servitude.

You came here because you were tired of being a machine, he reminded himself. He could almost hear Admiral Best's stern voice urging him to put this woman out of her misery, but who was he to say she was miserable?

Lukas had been miserable. It had taken him years to realize that, to understand that the military hadn't been able to program everything out of him that made him Lukas.

He picked her up, backpack and all, and slung her over his shoulder before starting the trek back to the command tower.

CHAPTER 2

THERE WAS little space for guests in the command tower, Lukas's home. He spent most of his time in the control room, but there was a large storage closet he'd set up as a makeshift bedroom. He didn't require a great deal of sleep and he could do it almost anywhere, so he didn't hesitate to leave his stowaway on the cot there.

You aren't going to kill her. He could hear Admiral Best mocking him as he laid her down on the cot's thin mattress and thought about where he could still find medication on Haven. He could run antidote programs should he ever come in contact with carnibo sap and he wasn't sure he could even get sick at all, so he had very little knowledge of Haven's available medical supplies.

There were several storerooms on the tower's first level, and he checked those after leaving her on the bed. One was full of dehydrated ready-meals that never expired, and he'd eaten more than a few over the years, and in another, he found some dusty dermosprays of carnibo antidote, which he pocketed.

On second thought, he checked the long-disused wardrobe cabinet and pulled out a set of black fatigues that would probably be too big, but at least they weren't covered in sap. He draped them over his arm and headed back for the metal spiral staircase that would take him back to his home at the top of the tower. Halfway up the stairs, he stopped.

Would he have to undress her to get her away from all that sap?

He swallowed. *No, I can't do that.*

Lukas wasn't a medic, beyond the rudimentary lifesaving skills he'd been taught in basic training.

He'd give her some of the antidote, he decided, then she could wake up, clean herself off, and he would give her more medication if necessary.

Killing her would have been easier.

Now that she was here, in his sanctuary, he didn't know if he'd made the right decision.

Cressida stirred, and it was a fight to open her eyes and raise her head. Her vision swam.

She was on something soft. *Definitely not the ground.*

Memories came flooding back: the *Gryphon*, the attendant she'd bribed so she could look outside, the sight of Haven.

The tree and finding herself coated in sap. Thorns piercing her on all exposed areas.

Oh, God, the Gryphon...

She was not on board a ship right now; there wasn't the reassuring purr of engines beneath her.

Which meant she was still on Haven.

They left me behind.

She hauled herself up, panic coursing through her. She was in a small, unfamiliar room, a single light flickering from a panel in the ceiling. There was an open doorway a meter or so away from the cot she'd been placed on.

"Hello?" Her voice held a shrill edge to it, and she fought the urge to scream and cry.

Footsteps sounded from somewhere in the next room, and a tall figure quickly filled the doorway. "You're awake."

The voice was unfamiliar, male, and deep. Fear snaked its way down Cressida's spine.

Haven was supposed to be an uninhabited planet. The only thing that could possibly be worse than being marooned on an uninhabited planet was being marooned with a strange man.

Tears sprang to Cressida's eyes. "Please don't hurt me." She damned the squeak in her voice and raised her hand to wipe away tears, her muscles screaming in protest.

Faster than she thought possible, the stranger was beside the bed and holding her hand away from her face with a black-gloved one of his own. "Don't do that," he said. "You'll pass out again."

There was a trace of something odd in his voice, the vocal equivalent of rust, Cressida thought. Like he hadn't used his voice in a very long time. "Who are you?"

He didn't relinquish his grip on her wrist. "Just call me Lukas. You need to wash off that sap. I have a change of clothes for you."

"I need to get in touch with the *Gryphon*," she said. "Where is it?"

"Long gone."

A wail escaped her, involuntarily. "I'm trapped here?"

"It would seem so. Believe me, I'm not happy about it either." He released her hand. "I can draw a bath for you in hydroponics. Get out of bed carefully and hold your arms away from you."

Cressida's brain tried to process everything that had just happened. "What do you mean about the sap?"

"You were covered in carnibo sap. It's a neurotoxin found in the deciduous trees around the launch pad."

Of course, Cressida would choose a poisonous tree to jump on. "Oh."

Irritation crept into his voice. "Get up."

She complied, not knowing what else to do. "How long have you been here, Lukas?"

He paused before replying. "Almost six years."

How the hell had he survived that long? She wanted to ask him, but judging from his voice and demeanor he wasn't up for any further conversation.

His earlier words echoed in her mind. *I'm not happy about it, either.*

That didn't bode well for Cressida.

Her joints were stiff when she found her footing, but she followed him into a larger room covered in comp thinscreens and command boards, all of them dark. There were large windows on three sides, the grimy plastiglas revealing an overcast sky and treetops. She could see crumbling structures in the distance.

Lukas turned around, and she now she could see his face clearly. Slashes of dark brows were knitted together over equally dark eyes as he took her in, holding her sticky arms away from her body, his lips downturned in... what? Disapproval, she supposed. She could hardly blame him.

His crudely-cut dark hair revealed a small port on his right temple, and she could see scars running along his jaw and down his neck, at least what was visible under the high collar of the faded black fatigue shirt he wore. It matched his pants and boots, also black.

He's a cyborg!

Her eyes fixed on his temple port and she had to force herself to look away. From the way his lips thinned, he must have noticed but didn't comment on her perusal. "Follow me," he said. "Watch your step."

She stiffly followed him down a spiral staircase that wound through whatever structure they were in, and outside. It was chillier than Cressida was used to, but she was also accustomed to living and working on a climate-controlled planet. Marooned or not, the unfiltered air was a novelty to her. At least she didn't have to pay for that here.

They walked past small, dilapidated huts that probably served as barracks at one point, and a few other, larger buildings whose purposes Cressida couldn't guess. When she looked over her shoulder she saw the structure she and Lukas had exited: a tall, slim tower, devoid of windows except at the top.

"Hydroponics still has running water," Lukas called out ahead of her, and she picked up her pace in an attempt to keep up. It was hard to do when she couldn't move her arms.

The hydroponics he spoke of turned out to be a greenhouse, its windows dirty but unbroken. He held open a door while Cressida hurried to catch up with him. She already felt dizzy again, undoubtedly a result of that weird tree sap.

"There's a tub in the middle of the room," Lukas said when she walked in. The door clanged shut behind them, and Cressida could see rows of mostly empty shelves and the occasional pot of something growing. "Please take care not to harm any of the vegetables growing. I depend on them."

She noticed the *I* in there. Cressida would need food, too.

Another shiver snaked through her. "What are you planning on doing with me?"

He stopped walking and turned around to face her. The semi-darkness made him look even more menacing than a regular cyborg, not that Cressida had any experience with them.

But he didn't reply. "Come on."

She hurried alongside him until they reached the middle of the greenhouse, where a large metal tub had been set up, filled with water. A bottle of soap powder, a sponge, a towel, and a neatly-folded set of clothes rested nearby, a dermospray resting on top. "You'll want to get that sap off you," Lukas said again.

"Right." She looked around, but Lukas showed no indication that he was going to give her some privacy. "Um... I think I'm good."

"Use the dermospray if you think you need it. It's an antidote for the carnibo sap."

"I think I will, thanks."

But he didn't move.

Cressida sighed. "I can manage on my own."

It took a few seconds for those words to register to him. His eyes widened slightly. "Oh."

"Yeah." She blinked, trying to fend off sleepiness. "I won't be long."

"I'll be waiting outside."

"Thank you." There was one thing she'd forgotten, though, and he hadn't asked her "Lukas?"

"Yes?"

"I'm Cressida. I guess we're going to be roommates, so I thought you should know." She tried to smile. "I'd shake your hand, but ..." She wiggled her sticky fingers. "You know."

To her disappointment, Lukas merely nodded upon learning her name. "I'll give you some time to take a bath."

Well, at least she'd tried.

As soon as he was out of sight and she heard the greenhouse door close, Cressida stripped off her sticky clothes and pressed the dermospray to the crook of her elbow to combat the drowsiness that had again crept up on her. If Lukas came back to find her drowned and naked in that tub, she would die all over again from the embarrassment.

She stepped into the water and nearly screamed. As it was, a whimper escaped from her as her skin touched the freezing cold water. Tears sprang to her eyes and she couldn't even wipe them away because of that stupid sap still clinging to her hands.

She held her breath and lowered herself into the tub until she was sitting down, knees against her chest. When she was reasonably sure she wasn't about to expire from a heart attack from the cold, she forced herself to relax a little. Then she reached for the soap powder and sponge and scrubbed herself all over until every trace of the sap was gone.

I guess running water doesn't mean it's hot. She would have to ask him about that, as well as a host of other things.

How can I get home?

Why is he here?

He had to be a first-generation cyborg model or something. A secret project. God only knew how many secret projects the Zone oversaw.

She didn't linger in the water, jumping out as soon as she was no longer sticky. She toweled off, shivering in the chill, and dressed in the clothes Lukas left for her. It was a set of women's fatigues, she noticed as she slipped on the undershirt. At least the boots mostly fit. She spotted a rack nearby, another towel draped over it and hung hers beside it.

She left her sap-coated clothes to soak in the washtub and walked back through the greenhouse. Lukas waited outside, back to her and ramrod straight. He was at attention for a commanding officer who would never show up, she thought.

There was a set to his shoulders that told her he knew she was behind him, about to open the door, and she felt like rolling her eyes at herself. Of course, he was aware of everything happening around him, he was a *cyborg*. Being hyper-aware of theirs and others' surroundings was what they were designed for.

That, and war. And killing things, she thought.

She still didn't know what he planned to do with her. Nervousness twisted in her belly as she opened the door.

Lukas turned around. "Cressida."

There was no trace of emotion in his voice. "Thank you for all your help today," she said.

"You're cold."

"I'll be fine." She needed to find her backpack and dig out the comb she kept stashed in there.

"The water was too cold for you."

There was a slight shift in his tone like he had just discovered something new. It was the same for Cressida—the man was a cyborg. He probably wasn't even capable of feeling cold.

"And it's okay," she said, forcing herself to smile. His expression didn't change. "I still appreciate the help."

They walked back to the tower in silence, Lukas always a meter or so ahead, and Cressida took advantage of the time to look around the remains of the settlement. "How often do ships pass by here?" she asked, breaking the quiet.

He opened the door to the tower and held it open for her. "Yours was the third in six years."

And they hadn't discovered Lukas. "Oh, no."

"The first came here to look for me, the second was a scavenger ship, and the third was yours."

It was the longest sentence he'd said so far, and it gave Cressida a modicum of hope that she might not be stranded here forever. Unless... "Is there any way for you to get off-world if you wanted to?"

He must have taken a ship or shuttle here. If he was military then he would likely also be trained in heavy air flying.

But his answer left her feeling deflated again.

"No. I destroyed the shuttle so I couldn't leave."

CHAPTER 3

INDECISION WARRED within Lukas as he and Cressida ascended the stairs to the top of the command tower. He hadn't considered where she would live—and live she would; he wasn't sure anymore he had it in him to kill her—and the dilapidated tower was the only place in the former settlement he'd cleaned up.

There was also the issue of her getting off-world. The shuttle he'd stolen when he escaped the Zone wasn't usable, but it could possibly be fixed with the various parts that had been left behind when Haven was abandoned.

She wanted to leave, but if she did, she could easily tell other people his whereabouts.

I haven't killed her, he thought. *And if I'm not going to, I'm going to have to live with her.*

A rare bubble of frustration welled up in him at the idea. He'd come here to escape other people, and he'd been—well, not *happy*, but content on Haven. Or the closest he'd ever remembered feeling content. Lukas was certain that any ability to feel happiness had been programmed out of him as soon as he was sedated on that hospital bed at Caron Cybernetics and that first chip implanted in his body, ten years' prior.

He could set her up in one of the barracks huts that dotted the settlement and make himself scarce until she was rescued, which he'd already considered. He might have to fake his own death if it came to that, or figure out a way to make her swear that she would never reveal his existence to anyone in the Zone.

Part of him fiercely regretted reviving her. She might have woken up eventually, but if he hadn't meddled, she would have wandered around until she met misfortune or starved to death, or, just as bad, a rescue crew could have found her and then him.

Any way Lukas looked at it, he was the loser in this situation.

He was quiet until they reached the top of the command tower. Not wanting to discuss his background or reasons for ending up on Haven in the first place, he asked, "Do you think anyone will come for you?"

Her answer surprised him. "Unlikely, assuming anyone notices I'm gone in the first place."

That was promising. "Why not?"

"I thought you wanted me off this rock."

"It's not that," he replied stiffly. Wasn't that what he was supposed to say in such situations?

Why the hell should he care about what she thought of him?

"You want to know if anyone will come looking for me and then report back to wherever you ran away from that you're here," she said.

She was more astute than he thought, he had to admit. That was better than he expected for someone who ended up face-first in a double-thorned rose bush, smeared head to toe with a known neurotoxin. She was waiting for a reply, so he said, "Yes."

"You go first," she said, settling into one of the control room's two chairs. "Tell me why you're here."

"No."

She started a little at the sharpness in his tone but didn't prod further. "I was an admin," she said. "Freelancer, for the education department. All contract work. I saved up some money to do some traveling around Zone space, turned down the last contract they offered me, and here I am." She held out her hands like she was presenting Lukas with a gift. "As I was traveling third class on the *Gryphon* and I bribed someone to let me out, I doubt anyone will come looking for me."

"No parents or siblings?" Surely, someone would have to come looking for her. It wouldn't be hard to deduce that she'd been left behind on Haven.

"My sister might get concerned when I'm not around for her to ask me for money, but that's it," Cressida said. "And Valenna has to run down her list of marks she hasn't hit up for scrip before she gets to me."

What she had just described was so foreign to Lukas that he couldn't keep himself from asking, "Marks?"

"She's a darfin addict," Cressida said, her voice curt. "And she has no intention of changing. Believe me, I've tried."

He'd hit a sore spot with her; he took note not to ask her about it again. He remembered darfin being a scourge before he took off for Haven. "What about friends?" He stumbled a little over that last word because having friends was just as outlandish a concept as close family members.

"I'm a professional administrative contractor, Lukas. I worked sixteen-hour days sometimes. And I live in Center City on Echo-7, the cheapest planet in the system, but everything there still costs money. Working that much didn't leave a lot of room for friends." She sighed. "I'm stuck here until another ship needs to make an emergency landing for a stupid repair or you decide to go back to the Zone."

"That won't happen," Lukas said. "Ever."

She turned large dark eyes to him, shimmering with unshed tears.

Alarm clawed at him, another unfamiliar and unwelcome emotion. He changed the subject. "How did you end up in that shrub?" he asked.

She sniffled and wiped at her eyes, but didn't start bawling. "It's stupid," she said.

"Undoubtedly."

She shot him an irritated look but continued. "I bribed one of the ship attendants to tell me how to get off the *Gryphon* so I could shoot some holos. It's a hobby of mine," she explained. "At least when I have to the time for it, which isn't often.

"All the exterior doors on the ship were open on the lower decks," she said. "That tree was the easiest way for me to leave without anyone seeing me. I climbed down and passed out, and I came to in there." She pointed to the supply closet. She sighed, blowing a lock of dark hair away from her face. "The guy I bribed probably won't say anything anyway once they check my stateroom and find I'm gone."

Lukas couldn't help but stare at her. She had done something unbelievably stupid and paid an incredible, horrible price. He wanted to berate her for it, but something held him back.

Before he left the Zone, he'd heard expressions from his fellow soldiers that spoke of "not kicking people when they were down." Lukas had never given those words much thought; he was designed to be the pinnacle of physical fitness and military cunning, the perfect soldier. Cyborgs didn't fall or find themselves down. In the unlikely event he took a tumble, no one would be stupid enough to kick him.

But Cressida wasn't a cyborg. He was now forced to share his planet with her, and he knew now that he couldn't just turn her loose in one of the abandoned huts scattered over Haven's developed area. She'd probably wander off and walk into one of the quicksand pits in the wild areas or something, and no one deserved to die that way. "Why were you on the *Gryphon* in the first place?" he asked.

She looked surprised at the question. "You mean, why was a lowly admin support worker aboard a luxury ship?"

Lukas didn't know anything about that ship's amenities but didn't elaborate. "Yes."

"I try to take a holiday every couple of years," she said. "Save up all my scrip and visit somewhere new, you know?"

He didn't, having only traveled with the military to war zones, but he nodded anyway.

"I was on my way home from the Toralian Belt," she said. "I spent two weeks there taking jungle tours and that kind of thing. Typical tourist stuff."

Again, Lukas didn't have any experience by which to assess that.

"I was supposed to go back to work in two days," she said. Her voice held little regret for that, at least. A watery sigh escaped her.

She sniffled again, but Lukas didn't see an immediate threat of tears.

She tried to collect herself, pasting a tense smile on her face. "So, Lukas," she said. "Tell me about yourself."

Her words had all the impact of a bucket of ice being thrown over him. The mild curiosity he'd been feeling about her evaporated. "No."

Well, he was just charming.

Lukas had all but shut down after Cressida asked him about himself and left the tower he called home.

Shut down. Ironic words to describe a cyborg having a silent temper tantrum.

He didn't say where he was going, but she hoped it wouldn't be too far.

Cressida used the time alone to explore the tower a little, not that there was much to see. It had obviously been a control area before the planet was abandoned; the command consoles and thinscreens were still installed all over the small area, although they were dark. She found a thinscreen devoid of dust with some cables dangling from it and gently tapped it.

It lit up, and the words *PLEASE CONNECT MANUALLY* flashed across it. When Cressida tapped it again, nothing else happened.

She picked up the cables, wondering for half a second what they were used for before she remembered Lukas was a cyborg. He was bound to have ways to connect to it. She dropped the cables and resumed her snooping. It wasn't like she knew how to break into the hardware and send out a galaxy-wide SOS.

Not that there was much to look at. Lukas either had the most boring life imaginable on Haven, or he'd carefully hidden any personal effects. Cressida didn't know which was more likely. He must've had something from his old life tucked away.

What am I doing?

She wasn't usually one to go poking around someone else's business, so why was she doing that now? She had to share living space with the guy. It wouldn't do to irritate him further.

Cressida wandered outside, and more clouds knit themselves together in the overcast sky. She needed to find out where Lukas had stashed her backpack if nothing else. Her hair desperately needed to be brushed and she had a travel sized grooming kit in it.

There was a well-worn footpath that followed the distance between the tower and the greenhouse, and less-used ones that branched off to other, smaller buildings. Their windows were thick with grime where they hadn't been boarded up. The sight was eerie, and Cressida didn't want to go looking in them alone if she didn't have to.

So she wandered around the buildings, keeping the tower in her line of vision, and waited for Lukas to return.

Lukas stalked through the ruins of Haven, trying to walk off the discomfort that wrapped around him, heavy as an overcoat.

He couldn't even articulate why he was so angry. His unwelcome companion was bound to have questions about him, was going to want to talk.

What a lonely life she had been living.

No family worth mentioning, no real friends. Granted, Lukas hadn't had any of that before he went AWOL, but he hadn't minded. The presence of other people in his experience meant pain and misery. It meant being crammed into a jail cell-sized living space because cyborgs weren't supposed to require more than that. It meant not being regarded as human anymore.

The Zone's military cyborg program, in his estimation, was the worst task ever undertaken in their history. He hoped it had been discontinued since he went AWOL.

Don't think about the cyborg program. Anything but that.

Try as he might, his cybernetics couldn't force his mind away from unpleasant topics whenever he wanted. Bitter echoes raced through his mind at the words his father used, the threats, when he was a teenager before he underwent the cyborg surgeries. His father had pleaded and cajoled with

Lukas to just consent to the surgery with a minimum of fuss, not that Lukas had ever truly had a say in it. He'd been destined to be half computer since before he was born.

Admiral Best just wouldn't have been able to handle the embarrassment that a disobedient son who didn't want to be a cyborg would have brought on him.

Lukas closed his eyes and concentrated as he pushed aside the thought of his father, focusing on Cressida and their predicament.

He needed to be kind to Cressida, he realized. He'd tried to before with the bath, sort of, although that had failed somewhat given how cold the water was. It hadn't been intentional. Lukas rarely thought about temperature since his cybernetics could control his own with merely a thought.

He'd come to Haven because he was tired of being treated like a cold, unfeeling machine. Now, he realized he didn't know how to act otherwise. Not that he did before he left the Zone, either, but he didn't have any reason to.

She was undoubtedly waiting for him back at the command tower. He hoped to the universe that she wasn't crying. None of his programming or personal experience could help him out with that.

He sighed, turned around, and walked back to the tower.

She wasn't there when he returned, and a mild thread of worry unwound through him as he searched it. The storage lockers holding old uniforms had been opened, and an energy bar taken from the rations on the first floor missing. He wouldn't begrudge her that. Military-issue, non-perishable energy bars were nearly inedible, even to a cyborg who wasn't supposed to care about taste. The food that was left behind was the primary reason he'd set up the hydroponics in the first place.

He could discern her boot prints in the dusty ground and he followed them, assuming she wouldn't venture very far from the command tower. At least, he hoped she didn't. He didn't feel like searching the base only to find out she was injured.

Why do I care what happens to her? She invaded my space.

He followed the prints that wound around the huts. Even though he knew the boots he'd found for her were too big, her feet still seemed tiny to him.

Because you came here to be a human for the first time in ten years and this is what humans do.

If Lukas couldn't bring himself to kill her, he was going to have to look out for her.

Cressida walked to a collapsed thermowire fence, its charge long since shut off, and stopped. Beyond the fence was an even more depressing landscape than the abandoned settlement: more carnibo sap trees, more double-thorned rose bushes and other flora she couldn't identify, and dark, tarry pools. A broken sign rested in the thermowire that screamed DANGER BEYOND THE FENCE in several languages. She didn't know what all of those dangers were, and she didn't want to find out. What was the likelihood that Lukas could come to her rescue twice in one day?

Another, more ominous, thought struck her. Would Lukas even want to?

She turned around and started back for the tower. She stopped in her tracks at the sight of the cyborg five or so meters away.

Both of them stared at one another for a few seconds. Finally, Cressida raised her hand and gave him a small wave. "Hi."

He nodded in response.

She crossed the short distance to him. "I didn't even hear you."

"I'm stealthy," he said. "It goes with being a cyborg."

His expression remained neutral, but she had the sense that he was trying to be nice. She should do so likewise. "I'm sorry I asked you so many questions before." She looked away and fixed her gaze on a piece of damaged thermowire.

"No apologies are necessary. I overreacted. I haven't dealt with other people for a very long time." She met his eyes, and he nodded to the area beyond the fence. "Don't leave the settlement. There are quicksand pits and natural predators out there."

Alarm flared in Cressida, and she remembered what her thincomp told her about Haven's flora and fauna. She'd already seen firsthand what the flora could do. "Predators?"

"They're mostly reptilian," Lukas said as if that made things better. "Haven has ten known species of venomous birds, lizards, and snakes, including seventeen known subspecies. Fortunately, they're nocturnal."

Cressida couldn't keep a shudder from escaping her. "So you're saying I was lucky I only ran into some toxic sap instead of a snake."

"Yes. The military didn't leave a lot of antidotes when they abandoned the planet." She heard the subtext loud and clear: *I can't save you if you're stupid enough to wander away from the base.*

Lukas continued, "I simply stay inside the command tower after dark."

They started walking back to the tower, boots whispering over dirt. "That's what I guessed it was." Cressida nodded in the structure's direction, still visible over the crumbling rooftops.

"Yes. Its equipment monitored everything on the planet,"

he said. "Air traffic, communications, weather patterns, climate, rations."

"And most of that doesn't work now," she said softly, thinking of communications.

"No," he said, his voice hard. "It doesn't."

"But you can hook yourself up to the comps and see stuff, right?" If he could do that, there must be a way for him to fix something just enough so she could send out an SOS.

"I have limited abilities in that area, but I can't repair anything I don't have replacement parts for. Most of the equipment was stripped out before I arrived."

Cressida could taste the disappointment and despair as acutely as that horrible ration bar she'd scoffed from the tower. She was stuck here, at least until another ship had to make an emergency planetside landing.

She'd lost track of the number of times she'd been threatened with tears, but once again, she forced them away. She was going to have to make the best of a terrible situation, and the first thing she needed to remember was that she wasn't alone. If nothing else, she'd lucked out being rescued by a cyborg. They were supposed to be calm, rational, and logical beings, weren't they?

She sneaked a look at Lukas.

Only Cressida would find herself on an uninhabited planet with a cyborg who'd gone AWOL.

She tried to inject a little levity into her voice as they walked toward the tower. She had to force herself to keep up with his long strides. "So, what do you do for fun around here?"

"Fun?" He said the word like it was from a foreign language.

"You know. Games or something."

"It's a lot of work to keep myself from starving to death, and now I have someone else to feed, too."

Well, that was a kick to the gut. "Sorry," she said. "Tell me what to do and I can help you." She looked around the derelict huts as they passed by. "Do you ever look in these?"

"There isn't much in them."

Of course, there wasn't. "Oh. Okay."

They kept on walking, and he slowed a little to match Cressida's pace. Neither spoke for a few minutes, but it was Lukas who broke the silence. "If you like, I can show them to you," he said. "For fun. Or you may want to move into one of them yourself."

"Are they even habitable?"

"They could be, with some work." His voice had grown a little softer, more understanding.

He was trying, Cressida reminded herself. God only knew what he'd been through in the military. Living smack-dab in the middle of Zone space—cramped, dirty, and very expensive—meant she'd been shielded from the worst of the territory war with the neighboring Brava System, and hadn't known anyone enlisted.

She had so many questions for him, but she already knew they'd be rebuffed.

They walked on in silence until they reached the command tower.

CHAPTER 4

LUKAS SET up Cressida in his makeshift bedroom for the night. He waited until her breathing became deep and even before silently moving away and connecting himself to the tower's comm array.

What he'd told her about communications being down wasn't totally a lie. If he really wanted to, he could probably scavenge the necessary parts to repair outgoing messaging, but doing that could also alert some faraway military body that there were people present on Haven, and could result in his being court-martialed.

A rare shudder rippled through Lukas at the thought of what prison conditions for cyborgs could be like.

Wires inserted in his wrist ports, he silently monitored the news reports streaming through the Zone, watching for anything about Cressida Merchant. The *Gryphon* would have certainly returned to port by now, and any news of ...

Ah, there it was.

The *Gryphon* had returned safely, although she was going to be stripped for scrap as the fuel lines were no longer workable. A lone female passenger was also discovered to be missing upon docking and mentioned Cressida's name, but no one seemed to be terribly worried yet. No family members or friends had come forward, although based on what she had said about her sister, Lukas wasn't surprised about that.

She hadn't mentioned her parents, he realized. Maybe he could ask her about them, find out why they weren't appearing in Zone news broadcasts, tearfully begging for the *Gryphon*'s parent company to conduct an investigation into her disappearance.

He could ask her about her parents, and he could offer some information about himself. An exchange, he reasoned. A conversation. Wasn't that what normal people did?

No one had tried to contact Haven, not that anyone would try to, and there was no mention of the planet in any of the news about Cressida. He disconnected himself from the comp and sat down in one of the two chairs he kept up here, his new bed until Cressida was set up in a hut.

But no one would be seriously looking for her. Hadn't she mentioned bribing a ship attendant to let her out? That guy wouldn't want to turn himself in.

He thought back to the fleeting mention of her on the news: *Cressida Merchant, aged twenty-six, was discovered missing from the grounded passenger vessel* Gryphon. *The Zone Authorities do not suspect foul play at this time.*

He remembered his own flight to Haven, those first stressful months where he was sure he was going be tracked down and court-martialed at any second. No, it wasn't even the possible court-martial that worried him that much; it was his father.

Admiral Best would have torn his own son apart, piece by piece, chip by chip, and sold *him* for scrap and donated any remaining organic matter to a tissue bank, with his own hands. Or he would have tried to.

Lukas had fled the military because he didn't want to have to kill his own father, which was what would have happened otherwise. He was tired of killing things and being berated for not being totally emotionless about it.

And he wasn't *supposed* to dislike killing things. It was something he was supposed to do automatically. He'd been bred and built for it.

He leaned back in his chair, a creak issuing from it. He cringed at the noise and waited for Cressida to wake up, but he heard her roll over and her deep breathing resumed.

He didn't begrudge her the cot. He didn't even mind her sharing the tower with him, at least for now. In fact, now that he thought about it, having a friend on the planet might not be so bad.

Friend. He'd never had one before. But if this was going to work, he was going to have to be nice to her.

He would have to make her not want to leave Haven, even if the opportunity presented itself. Whatever happened, he would not return to the Zone.

Cressida woke up with a stiff neck and a stomach gnawing at itself with hunger. *How the hell does Lukas live on so little food?* She'd had no idea that cyborgs required so little.

He wasn't in the control room when she left the sleeping area, so she let herself out of the tower and into the gray day outside to the greenhouse. "Lukas?" she called.

Its door opened, and he emerged with a handful of ground apples and beron nuts. He looked surprised to see her. "You're awake?"

"Good morning to you, too." God, she could really use a cup of coffee. She wouldn't get any as long as she stayed on Haven, though. She tried not to sigh at the thought.

He held his hands out. "I brought breakfast."

She could have launched herself at him and snatched everything out of his hands at those words. "Thank you."

"They aren't native to Haven," he said as if that had been on her mind. "Seeds were left behind. I cultivated them."

There was a touch of pride in his voice, but Cressida barely noticed it as he handed a bright green ground apple to her, gloved fingers brushing against hers. A frisson of electricity zinged through her at the contact, sending her nerves on alert. If she hadn't known any better, she could have sworn he'd done a cyborg thing.

His dark eyes fixed on hers, but she didn't read anything malicious there. Still, it was a few seconds before either of them looked away.

Huh. Weird.

She accepted a pair of the large, shiny black striped beron nuts, sticking them in her jacket pocket for later. Lukas took a bite of his ground apple and motioned ahead. "There's a hut that I think will work for your purposes. It's intact and insulated. Haven has a short but very cold winter season."

Chewing her own ground apple, she followed him. The hut he held the door open to was perhaps thirty meters from the command tower and close to the greenhouse.

It was dusty inside, but as Lukas said, it was still livable. It was a one-room hut, with a two-piece lav off the side. "I connected it to the water supply earlier this morning," he said. "But you'll still have to use the greenhouse for baths."

"No shower units?"

"No." Once again, his voice was abrupt, and she wondered what nerve she'd managed to get on this time. That question was answered when he said, "There was a shower area for the full humans who lived here, but protocols said cyborgs were to be simply hosed off outside." He opened the lav door for her to look inside. "I was the only cyborg at the time."

She felt her eyes widen. "Lukas, that's horrible. I had no idea ..."

"Most people don't. And those who do, don't care." He walked the length of the small space. "We can clean and air this out, and I'll find a sleeping bag for you."

She was reminded of something else she needed. "My backpack," she said. "Do you know where it is?" She sat down on the bare cot, sending a small puff of dust into the air.

"I removed your belongings from it and tried to clean the backpack, but I'm not sure all the sap can be removed. Your things are in the hydroponics."

"But my thincomp and holographer are all right?" And her travel grooming kit. She really needed her hairbrush about now.

"I didn't check their functions, but they were inside and free of sap, yes."

She let out a sigh of relief she hadn't realized she was holding. "Oh, thank God." If she had her holographer and thincomp she could stave off any insanity for a while.

She finished eating the ground apple's spiral core and pulled one of the beron nuts from her pocket. She easily peeled it and tossed the black-striped skin into a dusty wastebasket.

"Is there any chance the military left behind any vids or music files?" she asked.

"Possibly in the command tower's archives, but cyborgs rarely have any use for entertainment."

He was making this difficult, wasn't he? She tried again. "You must have a hobby that keeps you from going stir-crazy here."

He paused, and Cressida knew she'd hit another raw nerve. She hoped he wouldn't shut down on her again. "I exercise," he said. "I maintain the hydroponics. As I told you earlier, it's a lot of work to stay alive on Haven."

"I have some vid and music files on my thincomp. We can watch or listen to them together. Because I'm making this clear right now, Lukas, that I will not be able to just exercise and garden for the rest of my life."

Or at least until she devised a way to send an SOS, or another ship broke atmosphere for a repair.

You're a cubicle drone, she reminded herself. *If you had the skill set required to fix the command tower without pissing off Lukas…*

But she didn't, which meant she was stuck here until someone rescued her by chance.

"I don't believe I've seen a vid for entertainment since I was a boy," Lukas said.

"Well, I have maybe a hundred of them saved on my thincomp. There must be a way to project the screen somehow so we can both watch. Mine's cracked. Do you think you would like musicals?"

"The last vid I remember watching for amusement featured anthropomorphic singing animals and I enjoyed it, so possibly."

He must have been really little when he watched that. A wave of sadness that had nothing to do with her own predicament washed over Cressida over the notion that the last time Lukas did anything enjoyable would have been when he was a kid.

She knew not to ask him about that directly, so she said, "I'm sure I'll have something you'll like."

He gave her a half-shrug to that comment. "As you can tell, I won't be picky." He finished the last bites of his ground apple. "Will this be sufficient for your needs?"

"Of course. You went to a lot of work for this, and I appreciate it. Thank you."

He twisted the hand crank on the hut's lone window to open it. "Just remember to stay inside at night. The thermowire fence doesn't do much to keep out nocturnal reptiles."

"I won't forget."

"And avoid the quicksand pits."

"Got it."

He moved away from the window and looked at her again, dark eyes inscrutable. She shifted on the cot. "This must be very different from what you're used to."

He'd been concerned about *that*? Cressida wanted to laugh. "I'm guessing you didn't spend a lot of time on any of the inner Zone worlds."

He stumbled a little over his next words. "My family is from Garshan, so I did."

Cressida was surprised to hear that he was raised on that planet, home to well-connected, old-money families active in the political and military spheres. Lukas's expression shifted a little at the sight of her widened eyes and he didn't elaborate, and she didn't ask. He would tell her when he was ready to.

Instead, she said, "I'm from Echo-7."

"I've never been."

"You aren't missing much," she said. "It's overflowing with working stiffs like me. The entire planet feels like a giant filthy insect hive, full of tiny apartments that cost too much for what you get. My air and water bills are outrageous and I can't afford to keep a personal shuttle of my own, so I'm stuck commuting on overcrowded passenger transports to get to work twelve or sixteen hours a day at a company where I'm not even a permanent employee." She hadn't meant to say all of that, but now that she had, she realized she didn't miss her old life just yet, just its conveniences and predictability.

Now it was Lukas's turn to look surprised. "Sorry," she said. "I didn't mean to unload on you. I like this, I do." She looked around. "Would you believe this hut is bigger than my apartment in Center City?"

"Seriously?"

"Yeah, and it'll be quieter, too. The block I live in is full of shift workers, and no one's ever quiet." She took the other beron nut from her pocket and peeled it. "I'm sure by now my sister's broken in and pawned all my stuff, but it's not like I had a lot, anyway." She tossed the skin in the wastebasket and broke the nut in half, popping a piece in her mouth.

"You seem to be in better spirits since I showed this to you." He sounded pleased, or at least she guessed that was it. It was difficult to read a cyborg's emotions.

"Look, Lukas, I have to be," she said. "I can't spend all my time moping and crying. I'm used to working hard, even if it isn't manual labor. At least I can see the end result of growing things to stay alive. I can't say the same for being a cube jockey." She finished the rest of the beron nut.

"Maybe you'll be working fewer hours, too."

"Did you just make a joke?" She stood up and joined him at the window. There wasn't much of a view, just some brown grass and the side of the hut next door. His black-gloved hands rested on the windowsill. His gaze was fixed on something outside. When he met her eyes, she could tell he was trying to smile, like the motion didn't come easily to him. Which, she had to admit, it probably didn't.

"I suppose I did," he said. "If you've decided you're not going to sulk and cry, I'm going to have to develop a sense of humor and social skills." He moved away from the windowsill. "Let's get your things from the hydroponics."

CHAPTER 5

LUKAS HAD EXAGGERATED how difficult it was to stay alive on Haven, something he suspected Cressida noticed when he taught her how to tend to the hydroponics. He had already laid down the foundations of survival years ago, and what he had done was easily maintained. The real threats to Cressida's well-being had always been boredom and the proverbial cabin fever, things he'd never worried about. He hadn't been built to want to experience anything that didn't result in improvements in some way, whether it was to a comp system or his physical self.

And there was you *who was a threat at one point*, he reminded himself. He still hadn't forgotten that he'd considered killing her.

He missed her presence after she moved into the hut near the command tower, which he hadn't expected. He was also surprised to find himself staying up late, watching her hut through the tower's grimy window, making sure none of the local wildlife tried to enter. He hadn't expected any of the snakes or lizards to try since they tended to avoid people, but … he wanted to make sure she was safe. He didn't understand why he was doing it, but it was happening.

It was confusing and unnerving.

She spent her time between the hydroponics and her hut, watching vids and listening to music as she said she would, and occasionally wandering around the abandoned buildings. Lukas often linked into the command tower's remaining visual feeds, watching her from all angles as she explored her new home.

It was necessary, strictly to make sure she was safe, of course. He didn't want to follow her around and bother her more than he had to. He knew he wasn't the best company.

He didn't want to disappoint her.

Because that was what always happened before he went AWOL. On the rare occasions someone tried to speak to him outside of a military capacity, he irritated people with his lack of social skills and inability to hold a conversation about nearly anything. It was important that he not mess up this fragile friendship he had with Cressida.

She was in the hydroponics again, singing along to music blaring from her thincomp while planting ground apples and blue beans in long, rectangular trays. There was only one functional visualizer in the hydroponics, set in the plastiglas ceiling, and its lens was blurry with dust and humidity. It wasn't enough.

What the hell. He'd been avoiding her for the last couple of days, not wanting to bother her. He pulled the wires from his wrists and slipped on his gloves before leaving the command tower.

She was still there when he let himself into the hydroponics, back to him, military-issue jacket tossed on an empty shelf. Her tank top was a little loose, revealing bare arms. The readout in the corner of his vision reported on the sight before him, noting that she'd lost weight since her arrival.

Her long, dark hair was held back in a braid, and she pushed a few errant strands behind her ears as she spread soil in the tray before her. She didn't hear Lukas enter the hydroponics, and he held back, not wanting to startle her as she sang and danced a little in place.

He had to admit it was cute.

She turned around and jumped. So much for not scaring her. "Damn it!" she said. "I'm going to have to put a bell on you." She picked up a towel and wiped earth off her hands. There were smudges on her forehead and cheeks.

That was also cute.

"You aren't eating enough," he said by way of greeting.

She picked up a water bottle and took a long pull off it. "You came all the way here from the command tower to tell me that?"

He felt like an idiot. "No. My sensors tell me that automatically."

Her irritation was replaced by curiosity. "Really?"

He'd never been comfortable discussing his cybernetic enhancements, and he knew she wanted to ask about them.

He wanted to talk to her, and this was something she was interested in. He could do this, and he steeled himself for that conversation. "I see the data in my right eye," he said.

She stalked closer to him until her boots were only a few centimeters away from his own. This close, Lukas's sensors could pick out the scents of soap powder and earth on her skin and hair, could see the gold flecks in her irises. He could feel the heat radiating off her body, and if he concentrated, could hear the blood rushing through her veins.

Or maybe it was his.

It was overwhelming and he had to resist the impulse to take a step back and recover. He remained rooted to the spot as she examined his face, eyes fastening on his. "They just look like regular eyes to me," she said. Her breath tickled his cheek, and this time he had to move away slightly.

"You wouldn't be able to see the sensory implants," he said. "There are more of them in my hands, too."

She looked down at his hands. "So you could touch me and tell me if I'm getting sick."

"I could detect a fever or respiratory changes, but I don't have any formal medical training." The thought of touching her, even in a motion as benign as checking for a fever or broken bones, was foreign and a little exciting. He swallowed. "I couldn't make a diagnosis."

He'd always hated being touched. It meant more surgery, more pain.

"You're always wearing your gloves," she said. "Would it still work?"

"There are sensors in them, too." Although not as sensitive as they were when he fled the Zone due to wear and tear and no way to repair them. He also didn't want her to see his wrist and finger ports just yet, if ever.

She looked pleased with his offering that information but didn't ask any more questions about his cybernetic functions. "So what brings you here?" she asked, walking back to her trays. He already missed her closer presence and followed her to her makeshift workstation. "You've been avoiding me for days, Lukas. I thought you didn't like me anymore."

She was teasing him without making fun of him. He could do this, he could hold a conversation with her. He paused for a few seconds, watching as she buried a couple of seeds, and then she turned back to him, waiting for an answer.

"I'm sure you've noticed I'm not the most social person on this planet," he said.

"No shit. It's scary when *I'm* the best-adjusted person around."

"I came here to talk to you."

Her expression shifted to surprise. "Well, I was getting lonely, so I'm glad to hear it." She sat down on the hydroponics floor and motioned for him to do the same. "Sit down. Let's talk."

He did so, sitting opposite her. She handed him her water bottle. "Want some?"

"No, thank you."

Cressida kept her gaze fixed on him. "So, since you told me about your eyes, I guess you want to know something about me."

"That's what I've observed in people having conversations."

"And I'm guessing you didn't have a lot of them yourself before you came here."

"No."

"Well, what do you want to know?"

Questions raced through Lukas's head, and he had no idea what would be appropriate to ask her. Finally, he blurted out, "Your sister."

"Wow, you're going straight for the jugular, aren't you?" She arched a dark eyebrow at him, and before he could retract the question, she said, "If I tell you about her and my family, I want something else from you."

His breath hitched.

"Tell me about Garshan," she said.

He exhaled. He could do that. "It's a deal."

"Okay." She leaned back, hands planted on the floor and long legs stretched out ahead of her. "I'm the oldest." She sighed and looked up at the ceiling, where muted daylight was blurred by the grimy plastiglas. "My sister Valenna is a darfin user, as I told you. She has been since she was a teenager." She took another swallow from her water bottle. "Our mother died from an overdose when we were kids. After that, our dad kind of fucked off and neither of us has seen him in a few years. I tried to raise Valenna as best as I could, but ..." She gave a half-shrug. "I was still a kid, too. We were thirteen and eleven when Mom died, and Valenna started using darfin casually a few years later. She was a full-blown addict by the time she was fifteen."

She sighed and looked up. She didn't take her eyes off the ceiling when she continued. "I really tried to help her get sober. She's been in and out of different rehabs around the Zone but nothing seemed to work, and three years ago I all but washed my hands of her. She only comes around when she wants something."

"And you feel guilty about this." Wasn't that what people usually felt about downtrodden family members?

"No, that's the thing, Lukas. I don't." She barked out a short, harsh laugh. "I don't feel bad that I won't be there the next time she tries to hit me up for scrip or I get a call from a hospital. I stopped feeling bad about that a long time ago, and now I've just sort of ... moved on, I guess."

Her cheeks were flushed, and Lukas knew if he touched her right now, his sensors would pick up increased blood pressure. He stayed still and waited for her to continue.

"If she gets sober, great. If not, I've already lost her anyway. I'm not angry or sad, I just don't really feel anything for her anymore."

Lukas found himself shocked into silence by her admission.

Cressida had been trying to get him to open up since he found her face-first in those shrubs, had given him the strong impression that she cared about him. He didn't think she was capable of writing off someone so close to her.

She noticed his lack of response and looked at him archly. "Have you ever dealt with a darfin user?" she asked.

"No."

"You grieve for someone who hasn't died yet," she said. "And there's always an end to grief. I've reached that." She looked away and briefly closed her eyes, but not before Lukas saw a thin film of tears there.

He didn't think she was finished grieving.

But her voice was steady when she spoke again. "Okay, your turn. Tell me about growing up on Garshan. I've never been."

"I'm from a military family," he said.

"Yeah, I figured either military or politics. Although in the Zone those often mean the same thing."

"Are you familiar with Admiral Steven Best?"

She thought for a moment. "I've heard the name Best in relation to the military and government, but I don't follow Zone politics at large, just what happens on Echo-7. Everyone on Echo-7 gets screwed no matter who's running the show."

"Well, I'm Admiral Best's son."

He waited for a wide-eyed reaction, but none came.

"He spearheaded the cyborg project," Lukas prodded her.

Again, no response.

If she could talk about her addict sister, he could talk about his reason for existing. "I'm alive today because I was genetically engineered to be the best candidate for cybernetic enhancements. My father made sure of it."

Her expression shifted as she realized what he was telling her. "Your admiral *dad* made you into a cyborg?"

He nodded.

It took her a few seconds to respond. "Holy shit, Lukas. How old were you?"

"Seventeen when the surgeries were completed, and then I enlisted. I was the Zone's first cyborg success story." The words were bitter in Lukas's mouth, and all of the old anger and hurt over what he'd ended up as came rushing back.

"But you didn't agree to become one, though." Cressida's voice was quiet, understanding. "No one could make that kind of decision at that age."

"No, I didn't." He'd spent the next five years trapped in the military. Lukas didn't bother trying to hide his resentment this time. "Admiral Best told me from the time I was a boy that being the Zone's first successful cyborg soldier was my reason for existing. While I tried to convince him otherwise, he wouldn't take no for an answer. It would have embarrassed him."

Cressida stared at him, shock written across her features. "Oh, my God. Lukas, that's so fucked up."

"It's too late to complain about it, and in the end, I managed to escape." He had no idea whether or not Admiral Best was even still alive—the man had been getting on in years even when he was born—but he didn't have the means to check.

"How?" she asked. "That must have been the escapade of the century."

"Cyborgs are enhanced," he said. "Superior problem-solving skills and an ability to directly interface with comp systems. It wasn't as difficult as I expected it to be. I destroyed the shuttle I arrived in, and hid in a cave outside the base for the first few days. The military sent out a small search party, but they didn't stay here long."

"That kind of escape is the stuff they base vid-stories on."

"I'm sure the musical numbers would be sensational."

Cressida looked surprised again. "You *do* have a sense of humor!"

He thought about what he'd just said, and it occurred to him that the only times since he became a cyborg that he'd cracked jokes, albeit unintentionally, had been in her presence. "I suppose."

"So does this mean you'll loosen up and watch a vid with me sometime soon?"

She looked hopeful for the first time he found her in that rose bush. He couldn't keep himself from analyzing her features, but not for emotion recognition. He found himself memorizing her dark eyes and the gold flecks they held, the smattering of light freckles dusted across her nose, her full lips upturned in what even he could see was a friendly smile.

When was the last time anyone actually wanted to spend time with him?

She was waiting for an answer. "Yes," he finally said. "It's a date."

Cressida giggled at that before rising to her feet and checking the soil in a tray full of ground apple seeds, probably thinking he'd made another joke.

Lukas wasn't so sure he had.

Cressida had to give Lukas credit where it was due: he really was trying to be friends with her.

She could tell that it had taken a lot out of him to give her the small amount of information that he had about his past. There was undoubtedly much more to it and him, but she wasn't going to pry. As grim as their conversation was, she liked the dynamic they were exploring. If she had to be stranded on an uninhabited planet, disconnected from the galactic net, she mused, it may as well be with a friend.

She checked the soil moisture on a tray of blue bean seedlings with her finger and wondered where Lukas had gone off to since he left the hydroponics. *Probably not very far.*

And even if he couldn't identify it yet, she knew he was lonely. He had to have been as a kid, knowing his destiny had already been decided for him, and then as a cyborg, no longer being seen as human. Cressida shouldn't have been surprised at his lack of social skills at first, either. He'd been alone for years, and prior to that, he'd been treated like a thing.

She knew loneliness. All of the worker drones on Echo-7

did. They knew the bone-deep exhaustion that was the inevitable result of hours of boring busy work that didn't make an impact on anyone, the piss-poor wages to live on, the ever-increasing bills for water and air in their shitty efficiency apartments. Loneliness meant saving every spare cent of scrip so she could take the cheapest vacation package possible every year or so as a temporary escape rather than a chance to relax and unwind. It was having her holography hobby to keep her from losing her mind.

Cressida hadn't taken any holos since the *Gryphon* left her behind.

She brushed the dirt off her oversized military-issue trousers and washed her hands in the freezing water offered by the old-fashioned water pump in the middle of the greenhouse. She returned to her hut for her holographer, still amazed that it was fine after the adventure that landed her on the planet in the first place. She activated the small device with her thumbprint and it beeped in response.

Cressida spent the rest of the afternoon snapping holos of the settlement, taking in every broken window, every dust-choked weed she could. She finished her impromptu session with an early evening shot of the command tower, half-shadowed in the dimming light offered by the setting sun.

Lukas appeared in the window, a quizzical expression on his face.

Cressida waved and held up her holographer.

CHAPTER 6

CRESSIDA'S FOOTSTEPS echoed as she made the trek to the top of the command tower, backpack over her shoulder. "Lukas?" she called.

The door to his room was open, casting light from its windows to the staircase. "I hope I didn't weird you out with my holographer last night," she said. "I can delete that holo if you want ..."

She reached the top of the stairs and started. Lukas stood before her, shirtless, shock across his face. He held a black shirt in his ungloved hands, which Cressida could see were striped with scars, data ports in his wrists.

Neither of them spoke. Cressida saw a well-muscled chest and shoulders, and then a network of thick, knotty scars that ran across his body and disappeared beneath the waistband of his trousers. It took a few more seconds for Cressida to tear her gaze away to meet his eyes and the mortified expression there.

She immediately stepped away from the doorway and turned to lean against the wall. "Lukas, I'm sorry," she said. "I didn't mean to barge in on you."

She heard a shuffling sound as he finished getting dressed. "I came up here to ask if you wanted to go on a picnic," she said, the suggestion now sounding lame to her ears. "If you want to, anyway. I thought that there has to be somewhere nice to set up, and there's a brand-new crop of ground apples that need to be eaten." Great, that sounded even more pathetic. She was already getting sick of ground apples, hardy and nutritious as they were, but they were still better than the old non-perishable ration bars she ate for dinner. There had to be a way to cook the fruit, make it interesting.

He filled the doorway, blocking the light. She turned to face him, his expression inscrutable. "Picnic?"

"Yeah. I've done all the gardening I possibly could," she said. "I was thinking we could go somewhere, share some breakfast, and, um." She had her holographer in her backpack. "Look at my holos? Or we could watch a vid?"

She still couldn't gauge his reaction, but she knew he was embarrassed. "I didn't mean to invade your privacy," she said. "Last night with my holos or today. I'll make more noise next time."

"I heard you," he said. "You woke me up."

"Oh, damn it." Cressida had lost track of time for the most part since her arrival, only checking her thincomp when the light changed. "I didn't know you slept in."

He shrugged and adjusted one of his gloves. "I only require a few hours' rest a night, and I have an energy reserve if I can't." He looked at his wrist, its data port covered. "My energy reserve was tapped out."

Relief trickled through Cressida. He wasn't pissed off with her. "You needed some sleep last night?"

"I've been mostly awake the last few nights." He pinned her with a hard stare.

Because of her. Part of Cressida was concerned that he was skimping on sleep, but another part was touched, a little thrilled at the notion that he was watching over her. Making sure none of the planet's fauna decided to make her into a midnight snack.

When was the last time anyone had cared enough to do that?

"Thank you," she said. "And I'm sorry."

"Don't worry about it."

His tone brooked no argument, so Cressida changed the subject. "Do you know a good picnic spot?"

Uncharacteristic anticipation raced through Lukas as he led Cressida through the settlement. Haven was lacking in picnic spots, not that he'd ever had any reason to have one, but he had one space in mind.

He held out his arms when they reached the spot. "This is as good as it gets."

Cressida laughed. "It's better than I thought."

"Just be careful of the water. I think at this point it's mostly for decoration."

She looked up at him, clearly pleased with his attempt at humor. He was getting better at it.

The spot he'd brought them to wasn't too far from the settlement proper. It was too sparsely wooded to be called a grove, but there were a couple of trees and a large, dirty pond, its water crawling with an uncontrolled population of gorba beetles. Even Lukas, as unemotional as he'd been programmed to be, found them distasteful. "Just stay at least a couple of meters away from the water," he said.

"What gross thing lives in there, and will it kill me?" She shucked off one of her backpack straps and opened it, removing a folded bedsheet. She snapped it open and laid it on the scrubby remains of the grass underfoot.

"Gorba beetles. They're bloodsuckers. Is that from your bed?"

"I don't know what gorba beetles are, and no, I found this in a storage shed and it didn't smell terrible." She sat down and patted the space next to her. She took out a couple of ground apples and water bottles and looked at the bleak landscape ahead. "I think this is the least-worst view on the entire planet."

"It's a change of scenery, at least." He picked up a ground apple. "What else do you have in there?"

"Oh, just what I could scare up from the greenhouse. Some bean salad, but I couldn't make any dressing, of course." She poked through her backpack. "Some ground apples, beron nuts, and imitation chocolate bars someone forgot in the mess." She laid out each of the items. "Nothing too fancy. This, too." She removed a small red-sided device Lukas recognized as a holographer. It was an older model, its top-set viewer larger than the one he'd had as a kid.

"I thought I'd show you some of my holos," she said, shyness in her voice. She picked up a zip-sealed bowl of bean salad and snapped off its lid. "It's my favorite hobby. My *only* hobby."

Lukas swallowed his bite of apple. "I'd love to."

That was what he was *supposed* to say, wasn't it? The words came easier than he thought they would.

There was the vid she'd spoken of before, too. He was looking forward to watching one, and he didn't care which. He wasn't sure what he was looking forward to more: watching something for pleasure or spending more time with Cressida.

She activated the holographer and an image of a large, rundown building was projected through the viewer. It was surprisingly clear despite the device's age. As if she could read his mind, Cressida said, "It was my mother's. I've taken care of it since she died." She pointed to the image, draped in shadows. A few lights flickered in the building's small windows, and the front doors slid open and closed as people moved through them. Cressida paused the image loop. "That's my building," she said. "My apartment's on the sixteenth floor." She increased the image's size with a flick of her fingers and pointed to a dimly-lit window. "Right there."

"Do you live with anyone?"

"No," she said. Understanding dawned on her face. "Oh, you noticed the light was on."

"Yes."

"That's the way cheap rentals on Echo-7 work, Lukas," she said. "And on Echo-7, they're *all* cheap rentals. Lights are automatically cycled on as soon as it starts to get even the tiniest bit dark outside, so they can charge us for the power. I ran inside to shut it off as soon as I took this." She brought up another image, this one panning through a small, sparsely-decorated apartment. Lukas noticed a few framed holo-stills on the walls, featuring a much-younger Cressida and who he assumed was her family. Valenna looked a great deal like Cressida, and both of them resembled their mother.

There was very little decoration beside the framed holos. Lukas spotted a narrow, neatly-made bed pushed against the wall and a metal wardrobe at the foot of it. "No galley?" he asked. "Or kitchen?"

"Just a mini thermowave burner," she said. "No replicator, of course. I told you my hut here is bigger than the place I was paying for on Echo-7." She closed the image. "Want to see my holiday holos? I was on a jungle tour in the Toralian Belt this time."

Before she ended up stranded on Haven, he recalled. A twinge of shame rippled through him at the memory of finding her, and how his first reaction was to kill her. Cressida hadn't had much on Echo-7, but she had lost it all the same.

She was still waiting for an answer. "Yes," he said. "I'd like to see your holiday holos."

Dusk fell over their picnic area so gradually that Cressida didn't notice it. It took Lukas peeling his eyes away from her holos—now looking at the ones she'd taken of everyday life on Echo-7—to look up and say, "We need to get back. *Now*."

Cressida remembered the creepy things that slithered around at night and stood up. They collected their used dishes and the sheet and stuffed them into Cressida's backpack, and she placed her holographer on top. "I'm sorry," she said. "I should've realized the time."

"Don't be," was his automatic reply. "I usually don't miss night falling." He seemed surprised at himself that he'd done such a thing.

"That isn't entirely bad," she said as they walked briskly through the base. "I'm just happy you weren't bored by my holos." She picked up her pace to match his long strides. "You weren't bored, were you? You won't hurt my feelings if you were."

"No," he said, an unusual levity to his voice. "I enjoyed seeing them." He slowed down a little so she could keep up. "I'm sure you've figured out that I don't get to see slices of other peoples' lives more often."

Cressida held her breath, trying to decide how to phrase her next question. "And yours," she said. "Could you tell me a little more about you?"

For once, he looked thoughtful at the idea of talking about himself rather than angry or repulsed. "What do you want to know?"

"What are your limits?"

He was quiet for a few seconds, thinking. "I don't know. Pick a subject and I'll tell you about it."

What it's like being a cyborg? But she knew he would probably shut down on her if she asked such a thing. Would he even know what it was like to be fully human, anyway? "The military," she said. "If you're okay with it."

He actually sighed, a noise Cressida hadn't thought possible, and when he spoke, he sounded a little unsure. "I was treated like I was nothing," he said carefully. "And it was encouraged by my father. But it turns out you can't totally program human emotions out of a cyborg, as much as they tried."

The topic was devolving into something he was probably uncomfortable with, but he kept talking.

"They can fuck up your social skills," he said. "So they did that instead and thought they successfully reprogrammed me."

It was the first time Cressida had ever heard him use profanity.

"That's why I'm trying with you," he said. "I've never had a friend before." He looked straight ahead. "But you want to know about the military," he said.

"Lukas, you don't have to ..."

"It's all right," he said. "I was deployed to the Brava border during the war, although the government didn't like to call it that."

"It was a 'conflict,'" Cressida said, recalling the news broadcasts detailing the carnage. "Not that we were affected that much in the inner worlds." Life was hard and expensive whether it was during peacetime or not. "It never officially ended. We've been at a stalemate with the Brava System for three years."

"I did wonder if the war ever ended," he said. "Even with

government and military inefficiencies, I'm surprised it's been that long."

"I haven't been following it very closely," Cressida had to admit. "But the Zone isn't officially in peacetime yet."

"If ever. We're a people who prefer to divide and conquer. The Brava conflict won't be the last." Those last words were bitter and Cressida again questioned herself whether it was wise to ask him about the military.

He continued, "I went into the academy after I finished healing from my final surgeries and for the first couple of years I was the perfect cyborg," he said. "At least to the extent that I'm a machine. Everyone else who uses that term just has a few enhancements rather than half a robot body."

There was an ache in his voice that pulled at Cressida's heart, and beneath it, loneliness and betrayal. He was the only one of his kind. "Lukas," she said, but he cut her off.

"I was the first one sent into dangerous missions," he said. "Even when I was still an ensign, I went in with my commanding officers to scope out areas. I'm harder to kill and I heal very quickly.

"I was hit with twenty-two laser strikes during my last battle before I went AWOL," he continued. There was a faraway look in his eyes that Cressida had never seen before. "The locations of three of them would have killed someone who wasn't a cyborg. I was only brought to medical attention because I collapsed after my unit finally won that battle. And Admiral Best was angry when he found out I was seriously injured."

Cressida nodded, not wanting to interrupt him. As reserved as he was, as difficult as the topic was, she could tell he had wanted to tell this story for a long time.

"I was supposed to be infallible," Lukas said. "It turns out even cyborgs can suffer from devastating injuries. I underwent more surgeries to repair the damage, but the anesthetic medical administered to me didn't work. My body kept running an antidote program to clear it out of my system. So I had major surgeries fully conscious and screamed my way through them. It was the first time I remember screaming."

She wasn't surprised to hear that was what happened, but it was still horrible to hear. Cressida had only a shadowy knowledge of how the military worked—an overcrowded, poor inner world like Echo-7 was usually devoid of its presence—but his story fit in with the other complaints from veterans she'd read about.

"I found out later that the admiral personally told medical to not bother looking for an anesthetic that would work on me," he said. "He thought I was being dramatic."

A loud, inhuman hiss cut him off.

Before Cressida could look around for the noise's source, Lukas picked her up and slung her over his shoulder. He started running with lightning speed before she could register what was happening.

The ground beneath them zoomed past, but all Cressida was aware of was the heat of Lukas's hands pressed against her hip and the backs of her knees, steadying her. The hisses turned into blood-curdling shrieks and she closed her eyes to fend off a wave of nausea from being jostled around. She grabbed on to his waist and hips for dear life as he increased his pace. Dimly, she was aware of her backpack sliding down around her shoulders, but she ignored it.

"Bats," he said over his shoulder. He didn't even sound winded as he raced through the settlement. "They're out early tonight."

And they were probably venomous or carnivores of both, Cressida thought. All she could manage was, "Mm-hm."

Lukas swerved sharply to the side and yelped. "Damn it!" he said.

Oh, no. "What is it?" Panic laced her words.

"Nothing."

She didn't open her eyes until Lukas lifted her off his shoulder and gently set her down in front of her hut's door. When she looked up she spotted a couple of oversized bats circling overhead, leathery wings flapping. Another unearthly shriek sounded from one.

Lukas barged into her hut and grabbed her hand to pull her inside, then slammed it behind them. "Hopefully they'll go away soon," he said, moving to the small window beside the door.

"What's the deal with the bats?" Cressida shrugged out of her backpack and dropped it to the floor.

"Venomous."

"Of course they are." She slipped off her jacket and turned on the hut's battery-powered light. It wasn't until she could see in the semi-darkness that she noticed Lukas cradling his neck in his black-gloved hands. He winced and sat down heavily on the bed.

"Lukas?" Trepidation made her voice wobble. "Are you all right?"

"Just a small bite." He didn't move his hands.

"Oh, my God." She crossed the short distance to the bed and sat down beside him. "Let me see. What can I do to help?"

"I'm running an antidote program," he said. "It was a baby bat and their venom isn't as potent as adults, so I just have to clean it and wait it out."

"Lukas!" Cressida reached for his hands to move them away. "At least let me clean it. I have running water in the lav."

"It's nothing..."

"You were bitten by a weird-ass poisonous Haven bat! It isn't nothing!" She got up and went to the lav to soak a washcloth under the trickle the tap produced. Standing in front of Lukas, she put a proprietary hand over his own gloved ones, still pressed against his neck.

He glared at her, obstinate. She glared right back, trying to put as much authority as she could into the look.

"You said I'm your friend," she said. "Well, you're my friend, too. And while friends bring each other home safely after being chased away by a gang of man-eating bats, they also help out when one of them is bitten."

With some reluctance, he moved his hands away. Cressida tried not to cringe at the bite. It wasn't as small as he said it was, and the skin around the wound was an alarming shade of gray. Cressida pressed the washcloth against the bite and held it there. "Don't worry about coming into contact with the bat venom unless you have a cut on your hand," Lukas said. "The skin has to be broken for it to be effective."

She felt like an idiot at that statement. "That's why you didn't want me to help you."

"I also have my pride, you know," he said. "And I've been bitten before by adult bats and that's much worse. I'll be sleepy for a little while until the antidote program has finished running and then I'll be fine." He offered her a weak smile, a first for him in Cressida's presence. "I always am."

He was trying to add a little levity to their conversation, but Cressida remembered his stories about the military, how it was assumed that no matter what happened to him, he would always be all right. "It's okay if you need to slow down," she said. "Everyone needs that."

Her eyes drifted to the small port on his temple. He noticed her looking and she quickly averted her gaze away. "Want to know what that one's for?" he asked.

His voice had taken on a looser quality and he shifted further on the bed until his back was against the wall. Cressida moved with him, keeping the washcloth against the bite. She wiped it slightly and moved it away to check the damage. It was already starting to heal.

She sidestepped his question with one of her own. "Has the antidote kicked in?"

"Mm-hmm. It almost feels like a sedative, or if I've been drinking."

She leaned against the wall next to him. "You don't strike me as the kind of person who drinks."

"I'm not," he said. "For reasons that must be obvious now. But I've read about what it feels like. You didn't answer my question. Want to know what that port's for?"

"Cyborg things?"

"It allows a connection to my brain," he said. "If anyone wanted access to my memories, that's how they did it."

He spoke the words so calmly that it took a few more seconds for the weight of them to impact Cressida. "Oh, my God. You really didn't have any privacy, did you?"

"No, but that's hardly a unique situation to anyone living in the Zone. Your movements would have been tracked and monitored as well."

"But not my head," she said. "And the government stopped its constant surveillance of law-abiding citizens on the inner worlds a few years ago. It was a waste of resources." Not that certain parts of Cressida's life wouldn't have been monitored in some ways, like her transport shuttle trips to and from work and how she spent her scrip, but her building wasn't bugged.

"That scrip was better spent on useless wars," Lukas said. He gingerly touched the bite. "That's the antidote program talking."

"So you're a little drunk right now," Cressida said.

"I suppose I am."

"You can crash here. That's what friends let their drunk friends do."

He offered her another smile, and her heart skipped a beat. "You should do that more often," she said.

"What?"

"Smile," she said. "You have a good one." She hopped up from the bed. "Want to watch a vid since you're here?" She pulled her thincomp from her backpack and turned it on, setting it up to project the vid on the wall opposite them rather than watching the show on its cracked screen.

"Yes, I'd like that very much. Your choice."

He hadn't watched one since he was a kid, she recalled. She scrolled through her collection, picking a light, fluffy musical comedy before joining him on the bed again. "I hope you don't hate singing and dancing," she said.

He shook his head slightly. "I don't think I do."

Lukas's antidote program finished running halfway through the vid, and he was grateful to feel more like himself again. He hated the general state of dopiness antidotes left him in, even though he could control himself.

But now that it was over, he was very aware of Cressida's presence on the bed next to him, mere centimeters away; he could feel her body heat as acutely as he would the warmth of a fire. He felt like an idiot now for pointing out the data port in his temple while the program ran its course. What was the point of that?

He'd reminded her he was a cyborg, he recalled.

At least he hadn't told Cressida that he once thought about killing her or he was now forever grateful to the universe that she ended up on Haven with him. Or that he had already memorized her features, her smile, how she felt over his shoulder when he bolted through the base back to her hut. That he hadn't told her his first priority had been making sure that she was safe, even if he'd made an ass of himself while he did so.

The vid she picked had a storyline that was easy enough to follow, which was good since he had difficulty focusing on it with Cressida next to him. She drew up her knees, resting her chin on them, as she watched it, occasionally glancing over at him. There was genuine happiness in her expression again, something that warmed the place where he hadn't known his heart was.

He wanted to keep that look on her face always, but he didn't know how. He didn't have enough prior experience with people to forge relationships, let alone the romantic one he was already pining for with her.

He'd come to recognize what his growing feelings for her meant while the antidote ran its course and she fussed over him. It was nice, he thought as he watched the screen, to have someone care about *him*: Lukas Best, wayward soldier, rather than a robot. That had never happened before.

He thought, by the sparkle in her eyes when she looked at him, that she might reciprocate his feelings, but he couldn't be sure. He didn't know how to read those expressions. And no matter what happened between them, he needed her presence in his life.

What if someone comes to rescue her? He froze, eyes still on the wall on the vid's projection, unwilling to contemplate such a scenario.

He'd contemplated her rescue before, but only in a way that would affect his life should he be discovered. It was never about her or her happiness.

She would leave with his blessing, he decided. It had been weeks since she was stranded here, and by her own admission it was unlikely that anyone would be looking for her, but it was still a possibility.

He was unable to concentrate on the rest of the story, thoughts warring with each other, too many what-ifs. It was on the tip of his tongue to tell her what she was beginning to mean to him, but the words wouldn't come.

She stood up when the vid ended and stretched. "Lukas? What's up?"

I think I might love you, he thought, but he merely shook his head.

"Did you like it? I know it's super-girly and silly." She blushed a little. "But I like vids that aren't too serious."

"You get enough of that in your real life."

"Exactly!" She looked outside, through the window, at the total darkness beyond her hut. "You're okay with staying with me tonight? I know you like your solitude and your tower. I just don't want you to end up bitten or mauled by something else."

"I'm all right to stay here." More than all right.

"Are you hungry?"

"No." His nutritional requirements had already been met for the day and his cybernetics having taken care of the rest. Cressida helped herself to a ground apple from her backpack and scrolled through the thincomp's vid files with her free hand. "Thank you for looking after me tonight."

"You're welcome," she said between bites. "You did the same for me. It's the least I could do." She took another bite and selected another vid. "Do you mind if I start another one?"

"Of course not."

Another vid was projected against the wall, and she took her seat next to him again. Another musical, but Lukas didn't care about that.

A bat shrieked in the distance, making Cressida jump. "Sorry," she said. "I'm still not used to the animals here. Would it have killed this planet to have something cuddly and furry evolve?"

"I don't imagine there's much in the way of cuddly animals in the inner worlds."

"You'd be correct. Pets are expensive." She finished her ground apple and leaned against the wall, legs hanging over the edge of the bed. "How's your neck?"

According to the omnipresent data readout in the corner of his vision, it was fine. When he touched it, the sensors in his gloves picked up healing tissue and nothing else. "On the mend."

"Fast healing has to be the only benefit of being a cyborg," she said.

"The enhanced sensory abilities are helpful as well, but yes, I suppose they're positives."

Vid forgotten, she looked up at him. "How enhanced? Are we talking echolocation abilities or can you just see in the dark?"

"No to the first, yes to the second."

"What about touch?"

This time it was Lukas's turn to be startled, and it took a few seconds to find his voice. "What about it?"

He hadn't meant for the words to come out as husky as they did, but Cressida's eyes widened all the same. Her pupils dilated, something he wouldn't have been able to notice in the dim light without his enhanced vision and the data readout noting it.

"Can you feel someone's heartbeat through, I don't know, their knee or something?" She swallowed a little. "You can run a diagnostic through your gloves. Can you do that without it?"

He stilled, any lascivious thoughts evaporating. She'd seen him shirtless, the only person who wasn't a medical or military professional to do so, and still only seen some of the thick scars that disfigured him. She hadn't been horrified, but that occurrence had still been a shock. It was an innocent question coming from her, but he'd been on the receiving end of plenty of nasty remarks about his gloves, his body's abilities, and his appearance since his first surgery.

But she wasn't medical or military. She was his friend.

Without thinking any further, he stripped off his gloves and clasped her hands in his own.

It was his first skin-to-skin contact with another person since he was a child, and the air was sucked from his lungs at the sensation. Her hands were warm in his, her flesh smooth despite her hours of work in the hydroponics. Unconsciously, his hands slid over hers, memorizing every detail through the sensors embedded in his skin.

Sensors and data ports in his wrists. She had to have felt those.

He pulled away abruptly. A character in her musical vid started singing, but he tuned that out.

"Lukas?" she said. Her voice was curious, and he detected some dismay there. "Did I push you too hard?"

"No," he said. "It's me." He looked down at his hands, so rarely exposed, and never to another person. Shiny healed scars shone in the projection's light, and when he turned them over, he could see the silvery sensors embedded in the skin.

"What's wrong with them?"

"They're cyborg hands."

"I know," she said softly. "But there's nothing wrong with them."

Impulsively he reached for hers again, fingertips pressed against the undersides of her wrists. It wasn't the same as when he was wearing his gloves, but he could still feel her pulse beating, speeding up now.

Her breath hitched, and his eyes met hers. Lukas desperately wanted to kiss her at that moment, but couldn't tell if he was misreading signs.

He did not want to fuck up the first friendship he ever

had. Even he, with his lack of social skills and experience, knew that could happen.

But she didn't move away, and her heartbeat matched his own. "Cressida," he said. There was that husky quality again.

"Yes?" Her voice was breathless. His fingers stroked the sensitive skin of her wrist and she shivered.

I'm not good at this, he wanted to say but knew that would not go over well. His stomach knotted in nervousness and excitement, but he forced the words out. "Can I kiss you?"

She ducked her head slightly, a small smile on her face, and nodded.

His face met hers halfway. His heart stuttered at the contact, his body heated. When Cressida's tongue flicked against his lips, demanding entrance, his hands slid away from hers to cup her face.

His blood surged and body temperature increased according to his vision's data readout, but he didn't need those numbers to know how overwhelmed and out of his depth he felt. He broke the kiss and leaned his forehead against hers, trying to quell the nervous excitement that ran through him.

Cressida laced her fingers through his. "Lukas?" His name was little more than a whisper.

"Thank you," he managed to say.

"You don't have to..."

"That was the first time I kissed someone."

She pulled her head away from his, surprise on her face. "Oh."

She leaned in again, lips brushing over his hesitantly as if she was afraid of hurting him. It would be almost funny if it wasn't maddening. His arms slid around her waist and he leaned back, angling his body away from the wall to the end of the bed. She moved with him, levering herself up on her knees to straddle his thighs, mouth still fastened against his. She moaned and her fingers clenched the fabric of his shirt.

He pulled away, breathing hard, unsure what to do next. So he kissed her again, tongue meeting hers, encouraged by her breathy gasps. But a frisson of panic seared him when her hands found the seal on his shirt, and he grabbed her wrists, stopping her.

"Don't," he said, hating the pleading tone there.

He knew what she wanted. Hell, he wanted it, too. But not now. This was all too new for him.

"Okay." She moved away. His body already missed the heat and feel of hers, but it didn't change his mind.

"Can I hold you?" he asked. "While we watch the vid?"

He didn't care about the characters singing and dancing on the wall at all, he just wanted to be with her.

"Of course."

He laid down, back against the wall, and gestured for her to join him. She snuggled in next to him, back against his chest, and he wrapped a protective arm around her.

CRESSIDA WOKE up spooned against a warm body and felt a smile spread across her face. She turned around and faced Lukas, already awake. "Good morning."

She hoped he wouldn't shut down on her after last night.

But there was a warmth in his expression that hadn't been there the day before, and she hoped that meant her fears were unfounded. "Good morning to you, too."

"How's your neck?"

He gingerly touched the bite. "Back to normal." He paused, and his next words were a little shy. "Thank you for helping me out last night."

"We're friends." She levered herself up one elbow, and he put an arm around her to keep her from falling off the narrow bed. "That's what friends do." Realizing how that might be construed, she added, "I guess ... more than friends? I'm not sure."

"Me, neither."

She remembered his admission last night and knew she had to tread very carefully in the relationship department with him. As much as she cared about him, and he about her, this was all new to him. It would be so easy for it to get overwhelming and for him to close off again, on her and himself.

But he surprised her when he tilted her chin in his free hand and pressed a feathery kiss to her lips. As light and brief as it was, it set her pulse racing and desire pulsing through her veins. She had to remind herself to breathe, to not push him any further.

Neither of them said anything more while they got up from her narrow bed and stretched. To her surprise, Lukas was the one to break the silence. "Come back to the command tower with me and I'll make breakfast. I've been saving some dehydrated egg powder for a special occasion."

"I never thought the words 'dehydrated egg powder' would ever sound so appealing." She followed him out of her hut. "I need to take a bath sometime today, too." She and Lukas had figured out a way to heat the bathwater with some spare thermowire they found in a supply shed a couple of weeks ago. And there was laundry to do as well, although that would be a bigger task. She actually missed the constantly malfunctioning laundry machines in her building on Echo-7.

That, and coffee. But as she walked back to the command tower with Lukas, she realized those were the only things she missed from her old life. Life on an abandoned military installation seemed to be agreeing with her.

She sneaked a glance at Lukas.

Or maybe it was just the company.

True to his word, Lukas prepared some reconstituted egg powder on the hot plates he used as a stove in the command tower, garnished with sliced beron nuts and peppers from the greenhouse.

They ate in comfortable silence, until Lukas spoke up, his voice abrupt. "I don't want to mess things up between us."

Mild alarm threaded its way through Cressida at that

statement, but she kept her voice steady. "What do you mean?"

He parsed his next words carefully. "Cressida, I care about you," he said. "I've never cared about anyone before." He paused, not meeting her eyes. "Last night—I don't want to disappoint you."

She remembered fumbling for his clothes and his about-face. "You haven't and you won't." She took a final bite of rehydrated eggs, trying to put her own thoughts into words. "I don't want to scare you off."

"You won't," he echoed.

She felt herself blush. "Is that what you're worried about?" That he was a virgin? She should have clued in on that sooner. It would have been more surprising if he wasn't given his history.

"One of the things," he said. He didn't elaborate, but she guessed that something else was his scars. They wouldn't bother her, but he undoubtedly remembered her walking in on him yesterday, and she had to keep herself from cringing. God, she'd been a thoughtless idiot.

"We'll take things more slowly," she said. "It's not like either of us is going anywhere, right?"

He nodded and relaxed a little. He offered her a small smile, a gesture that came to him more easily than it did a few days ago, and one that set her insides fluttering again. When was the last time anyone looked at her like that?

Cressida's meager wardrobe was washed and hanging to dry on the various empty shelves and racks in the greenhouse, the most odious chore of the day. She turned on the makeshift heater constructed with thermowire and dragged the heavy metal washtub over it.

She looked at the tub and sighed. It was such a pain in the ass to fill it. But she did, pumping water from the hand-operated crank in the middle of the greenhouse into a bucket to pour in the tub.

She sank into the lukewarm water and ducked her head under it before reaching for the soap and washcloth before she heard the greenhouse door open. She froze.

"Cressida? Are you decent?" He was probably waiting in the doorway.

He was so freaking *polite* when he didn't have to be. "Define decent."

"Uh..."

She grinned. "I'm in the tub, but come on in." She stretched out, legs dangling over the edge of the tub.

He was quiet for a moment. She wondered if she'd crossed a line until he said, "All right."

Lukas walked in and sat down on the floor a meter away from the tub. His eyes flicked over what he could see of Cressida's form, and the distance between them didn't hide the way his pupils dilated. "I thought I would level the playing field," she said mildly, remembering the day before.

He shook his head. "It isn't level," he said. "You're beautiful."

A pile of ice cubes could have been dumped into the tub at that moment and Cressida wouldn't have felt it. "I should tell you that I find you just as attractive as you do me." She crooked a finger. "Come here."

He didn't need any more convincing. He moved to the washtub with inhuman speed, and she sat up. "Can you wash my back?" She moved her wet hair out of the way, then handed the soap and washcloth to him.

Lukas stripped off his gloves and rolled up his shirtsleeves. He ran the soap over her back and shoulders, his touch hesitant at first, only increasing his pressure when Cressida couldn't keep a small moan from escaping. His hands were hotter than the water she rested in, and she briefly wondered if it was a cyborg thing before deciding she didn't care. All that mattered right now was that he was here, and touching her.

"What brings you here?" she couldn't help but ask.

His breath tickled her ear when he answered. "I just wanted to see you."

That admission warmed her in a way she hadn't felt before. "In the altogether?"

He started massaging small circles on her shoulders and she leaned into him, wanting more. "That wasn't part of the plan, but it's a welcome sight."

"*Welcome?*"

"Unforgettable," he said. "I'll remember this always." He sounded a little hoarse, and she knew he was just as affected as she was.

Her breath hitched when she felt his mouth on her neck, lips firmly against her skin. He lightly bit the skin over her pulse, coaxing a moan from her. Her back arched involuntarily as his tongue traced a path to the shell of her ear.

"Where did you learn that?" Her voice was breathy, and she could tell from the way his own stuttered that he was just as affected.

"I'm making this up as I go along," he said. His fingers trailed from her shoulder down the slope of her breast, and her skin prickled in response. He hesitated for a second, likely gauging her reaction, before he touched her stiffened nipple, rolling it between his fingers.

"Oh, God," she gasped, head thrown back against his shoulder.

She turned her head around enough to kiss him, tongue tangling with his, her hands fisting the fabric of his shirt. She broke away, breath coming fast. "I'm getting you soaked."

"I don't care." There was that little smile again. She didn't think it would ever stop affecting her.

"Can you pass me my towel?"

Lukas did more than that, picking it up and wrapping it around her. "I also came here to tell you I have a surprise for you," he said. "When you get dressed, I'll show you."

Lukas led Cressida to one of the larger buildings in the base, one she hadn't explored yet due to its especially creepy appearance. She didn't believe in ghosts, but if they existed, they would probably hang out in a windowless crumbling, faded stone-and-plastiglas building on an uninhabited planet.

He held open the repaired door for her. Cressida peered inside, then at him, uncertain. "I've seen horror vids that start off in places like this," she said. "I don't like them. That's why I stick to musicals."

"It's better inside," he said. "I promise. I was able to fix something in here that I think you'll really like. Everyone needs a break from planting seeds in the hydroponics occasionally." He took her hand and led her inside without another word of protest.

"Lights," he announced.

Dim light flooded the area, which Cressida could now see was a large, black-painted room with rubbery walls and floor, marked with white grid lines one meter apart. It took her a few seconds to recognize what she was seeing. "This is an anti-grav chamber," she said.

"It is. Obviously, it was deactivated, but I figured out a way to make it usable," he said, a touch of pride in his voice. "The lights and anti-grav controls are voice-activated, although the anti-grav itself isn't that strong." He looked a little sheepish. "You'll only be able to get a couple of meters off the floor."

Cressida looked around the large space, temporarily shocked into silence. Repairing an anti-grav chamber with the scant materials he had on hand was nothing short of miraculous. "Oh, my God, Lukas," she said. "This is *amazing*. How did you do it?"

"I used some of that thermowire left behind and tweaked the power supply so it can run off solar energy," he said. "Not that we get a great deal of sunlight here, but it can respond to what little we get." He took one her hands in his. "Computer, decrease gravity, lowest setting." To Cressida, he said, "I couldn't get the comp to recognize percentages. The gravity's either on or off."

It was amazing. This had to be the most thoughtful thing anyone had done for her. Well, that and hauling her out of the bushes.

They began to float. Cressida couldn't keep a small shriek from escaping and she clutched at Lukas. "Sorry," she said. "I haven't been in an anti-grav room in years." Spotting the concerned look on his face, she added, "I like it, though." She let the controls lift her up about two and a half meters off the floor, and she felt herself relax. "Lukas, I love this. Thank you."

"You're welcome. I'm pleased you like it." He floated alongside her, dark hair sticking up a little around his head. She reached out to smooth it away, and his expression grew a little more serious. "I can't tell you how happy I am that I found you, Cressida."

There was that warm, squishy feeling inside her again. They gently bounced off one of the rubberized walls and floated back toward the middle of the room.

"I panicked when I first picked up your life form that first day," he said. "I didn't know whether to help you or ..." He trailed off.

Cressida had a pretty good idea of what his initial response to finding her probably was. "Put me out of my misery?" she guessed.

Shame crossed over his face at the suggestion, and she knew she'd hit a sore spot.

She gripped his gloved hands in his own. "Lukas, I'm not surprised. Or angry. You came here to get away from people, and then I showed up and spoiled everything for you. I would've been pissed off, too."

"That's just it, though. I'm not. I didn't know I was lonely until you were marooned here and kept on trying to be my friend." One of his arms wound its way around her waist and he held her closer to him. His eyes searched her face, and she saw pain reflected there. "I thought almost everything that made me human was either programmed or beaten out of me for a long time."

"I don't care that you're a cyborg."

"I know," he said. "You're the first person I've met since I was turned into one who doesn't see me as a machine." His hand gently circled her wrist and settled over her pulse point. In spite of the seriousness of his words, Cressida could feel hers speed up in proximity to him.

"I can feel your heartbeat," he said. "That's one good thing about being a cyborg."

"What about in the hydroponics?" She was grateful for the lack of gravity because her knees went weak at the memory. That brief interlude hadn't been enough.

"That was almost overwhelming," he said. "I think you nearly melted my sensors."

She gave a soft chuckle at that. He tucked a still-damp lock of hair behind her ear. "It was incredible," he said. "At least for me."

"It was for me, too," she said. "I like having your hands on me. I want more of that, Lukas."

He pulled her closer to him until her body was flush against his. "Like this?"

"Yes."

His hand drifted down her back to the swell of her ass, his touch nearly searing her even through the layers of her clothes. She hooked a leg around him to keep him as close to her as she could, and she felt him take in a sharp breath at the contact. She could feel the hard outline of his erection pressing against her, and it was her turn to gasp.

His free hand slid under her oversized shirt to caress her back, his fingers tracing small circles across her skin in an irregular, maddening pattern. She couldn't tell if he meant to drive her crazy, but he was doing it anyway.

More than anything, she wanted to be against him skin-to-skin. That would wait until he was ready for it.

"Tell me about your job," he said. "Back on Echo-7."

She'd hardly thought about it once she'd settled into her new routine on Haven. Her perpetual contract job at the cubicle farm now seemed like a distant memory. She remembered it the way she recalled stories her parents told her and her sister when they were children. She could picture her old workspace, but it didn't feel as if she'd really been there.

"Is this an information exchange?" she asked. "I answer a question about my old life, and you answer one about yours?"

"Yes."

"All right," she said. "I'll talk about the cubicle farm if you tell me ..." She thought for a few seconds, trying to think of a subject that wouldn't be too sensitive. "Your favorite book."

"I don't know if I'd call it my favorite, but *Zone Historical Offensive Strategies in Times of War* was helpful when I was in the academy."

"Damn," she said.

"Why?"

"You didn't even get a chance to read anything fun, did you?" They bounced off a rubbery wall and gently ricocheted back toward the middle of the room.

"No," he said. "I suppose not. Now, tell me what it was like working a regular job."

"Mind-numbingly boring," she said. "I don't think my job was even relevant. It was easier to keep the Zone's unwashed plebs employed at shitty, useless jobs that ate up all our time to keep us from revolting than not. All I did was alternate between standing and sitting in a cubicle while I tagged reports for management at whatever tower I was assigned to." She fought the urge to shudder at the recollection of the job's sheer boredom. "Contract work for government departments was the only job I was qualified for on Echo-7 after I finished school."

"Why didn't you leave?"

"Where would I go?" she countered. "I didn't have the education to qualify for a better job outside the Zone's inner worlds, nor the money to go back to school. There aren't enough decent jobs to go around anyway. Just the military, which you already knew. And I knew recruits were chewed up and spit out even before I met you." Although "chewed up and spit out" didn't begin to describe what Admiral Best had forced his son to go through for the sake of the military.

"What about your holographs? Was there a way to make money off those?"

It was sweet and a little naive that he thought she could earn a living off her holograph images. "No," she said. "I don't have any formal training or professional equipment, and it's just a hobby for me. Some people keep a written or video journal, I take holos of my life." She paused. "I still need to take one of you that isn't through the tower window."

His shoulders tensed slightly under her hands, but he didn't protest.

"So that's it," she said. "I tagged and filed reports for just enough money to live on and took a cheap vacation when I could afford it. That was my life. I don't miss it." She didn't. She had everything she needed on Haven to keep from going crazy: her thincomp and its hundreds of entertainment files, her holograph, a hairbrush.

And Lukas.

"Do I get to ask you another question?" she asked.

"Go ahead." He pushed off the wall with his feet, sending both of them gently flying through the gym.

"Any siblings?"

"No," he said. "And thank the universe for that. It would only know what the admiral would have done if there had been another kid to experiment on." There wasn't a trace of sadness in his voice or on his face when he spoke about what passed for his family. "My turn. Your favorite color."

"Really?" Cressida had mostly worn shades of gray and black; garments in those colors were cheapest and the most widely available. "You know, I think it's red. And I don't own a lot of red things. Just my coat, and the tree sap destroyed it."

"Your holographer," he said.

"Yeah, you're right. I had a red T-shirt on Echo-7, too. What about yours?"

He shrugged. "I'm indifferent to colors. Black suits me fine."

That admission made her a little sad. He'd probably been put in a child-sized military uniform as part of his brainwashing when he was a kid. She knew if she pressed it he would just insist that he didn't care, so she let the subject drop.

"What did you want to be when you were a kid?" he asked.

She had to think about that for a moment. "I'm not sure,"

she said. "It didn't occur to me that I could have any life besides living and working in small spaces. That sounded like a pretty good setup to me, actually. We moved around a lot," she explained. "Thanks to my parents and their habits. We were always getting evicted and twice a dealer came after our mother for money she owed them. I just wanted to be able to support myself, you know? And I did that." They drifted closer to the floor, then the anti-grav mechanism lifted them up another meter. "I did a six-month admin program at one of Center City's vocational schools after I graduated from secondary and I was mostly satisfied with my lot in life." Or she thought she had been, she mused.

"Are you happy now?" His gaze searched her face, and there was a stiffness to his body that she now associated with nervousness.

He relaxed and exhaled when she said, "Yes."

"I am, too."

"Did you ever entertain notions of being anything other than a soldier?"

"I wanted to be an engineer," Lukas said, surprising her. "Even after I was forced into being a cyborg and then the military academy—I always held out hope I could work in an engineering capacity instead of combat."

She nearly suggested that he could still do that, but held her tongue in time. He didn't have any intention of ever leaving Haven, even if he did have the means to do so.

And, she was beginning to realize, she didn't want to be anywhere he wasn't. So she was staying, as well.

"What are you thinking about?" There was his hand again, firm against the spot where her backside met her hip. "You're quiet."

"Nothing bad," she said. She looked around the room, still amazed by what he'd done for her. "This is absolutely incredible, Lukas. This must have been so much work."

"None of the athletic equipment was left behind, and the anti-grav functions aren't perfect, but..." He looked uncertain.

"Lukas," she said. "This is amazing, and the best surprise I've ever received. I love it." She pulled away from him, not without some reluctance, and vaulted herself off the wall they'd drifted to. "Now, see if you can catch me."

Lukas remembered to leave the anti-grav gym before nightfall this time, taking Cressida's hand in his own with a confidence he'd never experienced before. It was a cautious confidence, but there all the same.

"Join me for dinner?" he asked. He briefly held his breath, waiting for her answer.

"I'd love to. What's on the menu tonight?"

"Freeze-dried rations and blue beans," he said. "Reconstituted on my thermowire hot plate."

Her eyes widened in mock astonishment. "That's a gourmet meal. Lukas, you're going to all that trouble for *me*?"

His grip on her hand tightened and he felt a smile bloom across his face. The expression was coming to him more easily now.

That, and much of his nervousness around her was fading. Their interlude in the hydroponics was still in the back of his mind—would *always* be in the back of his mind, forever—and it hadn't been enough. The sight of her, shining naked in the tub under the lights, wet hair spread over her shoulders like a mermaid, and her invitation to touch her ... his heart stuttered in his chest and the front of his pants grew uncomfortably tight.

She wasn't repelled by the ports in his body or his scars. She *wanted* to touch him. The notion was just as intoxicating as that antidote program he'd run to rid his body of bat venom.

He held open the door to the command tower for her, waiting until she was safely inside before stepping in himself. "It's getting dark," he said, damning the tremor in his voice. Uncertainty threaded its way through his newfound confidence as he parsed his words for his next question. "Do you want to stay over?"

She nodded, a small, knowing smile playing over lips, and his heart skipped a beat.

I shouldn't be nervous. She had been receptive to him, even the initiator at times. His mind flashed back to the hydroponics, and then the night before when she'd reached for his shirt seal and he rebuffed her. He felt like an idiot in hindsight at that.

Whatever happened tonight, he would treasure it and her always.

She settled in the chair in front of the darkened comm panels as he prepared their dinner, refusing her offer of help. "Thank you for today," he said when he took a seat next to her at the comm.

"No need to thank me," she said. "*I'm* the one who's grateful. You gave me an incredible gift this afternoon. I can't remember the last time I had that much fun, Lukas."

He'd caught her during their impromptu game of tag, repeatedly. Although he suspected that was her intention. He'd spent the rest of the day since the hydroponics in an unaccustomed state of arousal, looking for any and all opportunities to touch her, and she welcomed every one.

They finished their meal in silence, and he wished he'd thought further ahead, maybe stopping at her hut for her thincomp so they could listen to music or watch something. Or even a bottle of wine, although he already knew there was nothing of that kind left on Haven. Even if there was, his cybernetics would filter out intoxicants, anyway. He just wished for some kind of distraction that would help him bolster his courage to initiate what he knew both of them wanted.

It hit him, full force, that he had no idea what the hell he was doing from here on out, or what she would want.

But she surprised him when she laced her fingers through his gloved ones, a mischievous look on her face as she closed the short distance between them and glided into his lap. He immediately responded, cupping her face in his hands as he kissed her deeply. She straddled him, molding her body against his, as her tongue tangled with his.

More than anything, he hated his clothing's confines. She adjusted herself on his thighs and his body roared in response and he had to take a deep breath to keep himself from doing something stupid. What that could be, he couldn't ascertain for sure.

He wanted her, more than anything in his life.

Lukas's hands were planted firmly on her waist, slipping beneath the hem of her oversized military-issue shirt. The data readout in the corner of his vision reported back her elevated body temperature, her increased heart and respiratory rates, all positive signs, but he still hesitated when he reached for the seal on the front of her shirt.

She turned lust-glazed eyes to him, breath hitching audibly as his hands pulled apart the seal, and nodded a little. It was all the encouragement he needed, and he peeled apart the seal and pushed the coarse gray fabric off her shoulders, revealing a plain black tank that was a little loose on her. He pushed a strap down her shoulder so one breast was exposed, and experimentally brushed his lips over it before taking it in his mouth.

Her hand on the back of his head and her harsh gasp was all the encouragement he needed. He pulled down her shirt's other strap, fingers grasping her other breast, spurred by her breathy moans. More than anything, he needed to be skin-to-skin with her, kiss and explore every centimeter of her perfect body.

He pulled away long enough to look at her, see the same lust reflected back at him, and he pushed her tank top up her body. She helped him peel it off her and it went flying somewhere in the control room, neither of them caring where it landed.

What's next?

Indecision battled in him; caught between his desire for Cressida and anxiety that he'd fuck this up. Before he could argue with himself or turn the most erotic moment of his life so far into something awkward, he stood up, lifting her with him so her legs were wrapped around his hips. She held on to his shoulders, and her giggle into his neck as he marched them both to his makeshift bedroom was another point of encouragement.

He gently lay her across his cot and stood before her, admiring the view before him. Her long hair was spread out over his pillow, pale skin soft and glowing in the dim glow offered by the control room's lights.

He wasn't sure what to do next. He paused for what felt like an eternity, although if he checked the data readout in the corner of his vision ... he willed that thought away.

Lukas didn't give a damn about the numbers scrolling past, refused to think of himself as half-machine for once.

She gave him an inviting smile, and his worries lifted a little. She wasn't put off by his lack of experience.

He hoped.

He kneeled on the bed, toeing off his boots, heartbeat thundering in his ears, and bent over her. She locked her hands around the back of his neck and pulled his face to hers for a kiss, and he relaxed against her, the heat of her skin branding him through his clothes. She released her hold on him to put her finger at his shirt's seal. He held his breath, waiting.

"Can I?" she asked.

She'd already seen him, scarred and hideous, and hadn't cared. He nodded after a second's hesitation. Her deft fingers pulled apart the dark fabric and pushed it off his shoulders, and he shucked it off with his gloves, not noticing where they landed on the floor.

His mouth crashed down on hers, in part so she wouldn't be able to clearly see what he looked like in the half-light. Her mewl told him he'd taken her by surprise, but she melted into him, body pressing against his and legs falling open. His hips settled between them, thrusting against her in a pale imitation of what he really wanted.

Cressida's moan at that motion dragged the breath from him, but he paused, hand gripping her hip.

What next?

She sensed his hesitation. "Lukas?"

He nearly told her, "I don't know what to do next." It would sound ridiculous because he knew what he was *supposed* to do, he just didn't know what Cressida wanted.

And it was so important to him that she didn't find him lacking.

But he couldn't form a sentence that conveyed that without sounding like an idiot. So he settled for dusting small kisses along her neck, her collarbone, to her the soft swells of her breasts. His uncertainty evaporated under her taste and touch. "Lukas?" she said again, between little gasps that spurred him on.

He lifted his head, and saw understanding mixed with lust in her half-lidded eyes, and couldn't lie to her. "I'm making this up as I go along," he finally said.

"What do you want?"

"You," he said, his voice hoarse. "Only you. *All* of you."

For the rest of their days on Haven, because he was never letting her go.

"And you're going to have me," she said. Her fingers drifted down his chest, skimming over his knotted scars as if they weren't out of the ordinary, to open the seal on his pants. "I want this to be good for both of us." She stroked his erection through the fabric and Lukas thought that motion might make all of his systems throw themselves offline.

He stilled her hand with his own. "Not yet," he said. This was going to be over before it could start if she kept doing that.

Now it was his turn, with shaking fingers, to finish undressing her. He fumbled with the clasp on her too-loose pants, finally sliding them and her panties off her and tossing them away, and sat up and propped himself back on his knees to admire her.

Cressida was perfect, and his hands skimmed up her thighs to the curves of her hip, past the dip of her waist to her breasts. His sensors committed the feel of her skin, her warmth, to memory, ones he would treasure forever.

He adjusted just enough so he could easily shuck off his pants, another wave of nervousness cresting over him as he did so. But Cressida's soft smile bolstered him enough so he didn't think she would care about the scars circling his legs, or the healed wounds from a long-ago battle that scored his lower body.

He settled between her legs, cock brushing against the heat of her thigh. That small touch sent a million sensations zinging through him and he paused again, trying to regain some control over his body and its reactions to her.

She slid a hand between them, guiding him inside her. Lukas froze for half a second, then he started thrusting greedily into her, their breaths and bodies in tandem. Her legs wrapped around his hips, urging him to move faster, and he couldn't keep himself from obliging.

She tightened around him as a harsh cry was ripped from her throat, the sound setting off his own climax. His mouth couldn't form words, as much as "I love you" tumbled around his mind. Instead, when the aftershocks began to fizzle away, he rolled on his side, taking Cressida with her.

He pressed a kiss to her damp forehead, breath still coming hard. She snuggled into his shoulder and draped his thin military-issue blanket over them.

Neither said anything as they lay tangled together in bed. Lukas thought she might have fallen asleep if she didn't keep tracing circles on his chest and shoulders.

He was the first to speak. "That was amazing."

"For me, too." She propped herself up on one arm, facing him. "Please tell me that isn't going to be a one-time thing."

The final tiny knot of tension he'd been carrying unwound itself at her words, at the confirmation that he hadn't totally botched her expectations. He gathered her back into his arms. "Never," he said.

The words he longed to say stuck in his throat. They may as well be in a foreign language, just as the idea of love was unknown to him until he met her.

He would say them someday, that was for sure. But not now; even he knew that might make things uncomfortable between them when she hadn't given any indication she felt the same.

There was affection in her gaze, and no hint of revulsion as she lightly studied the planes of his chest with her fingertips, a small, contented smile on her lips. That was good enough for him right now.

CHAPTER 8

CRESSIDA'S EYES FLUTTERED OPEN. Once again, Lukas was already awake, propped up one elbow as he watched her. Unlike the last time they woke up together, they were still naked, a state Lukas seemed a little less discomfited with. His initial discomfort hadn't escaped her notice the previous night, not that she cared about a few scars.

But *he* did, and she didn't want him to feel self-conscious about them.

She brushed her fingers over the scruff on his jaw. "I could get used to waking up like this."

He responded with a kiss to her palm. "Me, too."

She snuggled back under the blanket and curled up in the crook of his arm. "I don't want to get up yet."

"No need to." His fingers stroked her tangled hair. If she had been capable of it, she would have purred at the motion.

She was nearly asleep again when he said softly, "Is it a bad thing that I'm glad you were marooned here?"

Her response was automatic. "No. I like it here, Lukas. I like *you*." Her feelings, she suspected, were now starting to extend beyond liking and lusting after him, but she couldn't put those into words yet. So she tightened her hold on him instead, was pleased when he responded in kind.

"Well, you haven't experienced a Haven winter yet."

There was that wry sense of humor he'd been working on. She grinned. "I'm sure I'll make it through it just fine with you."

"I'd do anything for you," he said. "I mean that, Cressida."

There was an earnestness to his words, coupled with a more dangerous undercurrent to them. She had no doubt that he wouldn't hesitate to save her if something went sideways. Hell, she was there when he ran through the settlement at an inhuman speed to get them away from venomous bats, after being bitten by one. It didn't matter to her that he had a built-in antidote program. He still pushed his body to the limit to keep both of them safe.

Plus, he seemed to like the same kind of vids she did. That was an unexpected bonus.

"I'm glad you saved me, Lukas," she said.

He'd saved her in ways that weren't just the physical. He didn't have to rescue her after her experience with the carnibo sap, let alone set her up to thrive on Haven. He didn't have to extend friendly overtures to her, but he did.

She was lulled nearly back to sleep by his heartbeat under her ear when he said quietly, "No, Cressida, I think you saved me."

They enjoyed a decadent lie-in before finally getting ready for the day. It was late morning when they finally left the greenhouse, bathed and fed, but with little else on their to-do lists to stay alive for the time being. "What are we doing today?" Cressida asked. She fiddled with the damp ends of her hair, now fashioned in a long braid.

The washtub in the hydroponics hadn't been big enough for both of them, so they'd taken turns. Lukas had taken particular interest in combing out her hair, an activity Cressida enjoyed.

"We could go for a run," Lukas said.

She laughed, but another look from him told her he was serious.

"I told you when you first arrived that I exercise to pass the time," he said.

That much was obvious. She would have to be dead not to notice the effects it had on him. "I remember."

He'd watched musicals with her, the least she could do was reciprocate in an activity he liked. Besides that, she needed to stay healthy. There was a stash of various emergency medications left in the command tower's stores that would help her out if something—God forbid—made her sick, but there was something to be said for prevention.

Anyway, running could be fun with him. She remembered the anti-grav gym, the games they played there.

She took off like a shot. "Come and catch me, Lukas!"

He caught her, repeatedly, as they ducked around the settlement's abandoned huts. She even managed to coax a few laughs out of him when he did, a sound she didn't think she could ever tire of.

They ended up back at her hut after a couple of hours, although it didn't feel like just hers anymore. She liked that he made himself at home and pulled her down on the bed with him. "See," he said, "Exercise can be fun."

"Well, yeah, *some* kinds can be." She raised her eyebrow in what she hoped was a seductive gesture.

His eyes darkened. That must have worked.

"Running counts," he said.

"It was more like playing tag than running," she said.

"We still got our heart rates up." He laced his fingers through hers. "Yours is still is."

"You know damn well it's you that's causing that," she said, wriggling against him. She lightly bit his ear, and his sharp intake of breath confirmed that for her. "What else are you picking up from me right now?"

He'd seemed a little more relaxed about his cyborg functions around her recently, and she didn't think the question would cause him to cut himself off from her. But he didn't shy away from answering this time. "Increased heart rate and respiration. Your pupils are dilated."

"What's your diagnosis?"

"It's either a fever starting or you're *really* enjoying being in bed with me right now."

"Well, I *am* feeling a little hot and bothered."

"Hm." He looked a little thoughtful, but Cressida didn't miss the way his own pupils dilated. His lips brushed over her jaw, down her throat, to the skin exposed on her shoulder by her too-big shirt. One of his hands slid under her shirt's hem, the roughened fingertips of his gloves lightly tickling her.

He took the initiative this time, playing her body with a confidence he hadn't had before. There wasn't any uncertainty this time; Lukas was now a man who knew what he wanted. The notion sent another thrill running through Cressida.

He pulled her shirt over her head, then her trousers' seal before stripping off his own clothes. Goosebumps prickled along Cressida's skin until he settled over her, throwing the blanket over both of them. "Better?"

"I can't tell you how convenient it is that you can tell when I'm chilly."

"I thought you were hot and bothered," he said. He

draped one of her legs around his hips, his body cradling against hers.

"Can't I be both?"

"It isn't logical," he said.

"Not everything has to be logical."

"I've learned that recently."

His body pushed into hers, drawing a gasp of pleasure and surprise from her, and she thrust her hips in time to match his rhythm. Her orgasm hit her sooner than she expected, tearing a cry from her, muffled by her biting into his shoulder. When his body stiffened against her in climax, he held his position, dark eyes fixed on hers.

There was an openness there, one that extended beyond affection or physical attraction. In that moment, she knew she would never be able to let him go.

CHAPTER 9

LUKAS DIDN'T KNOW what shocked him out of his deep sleep: the ground rumbling beneath the bed, or the telltale boom of a starship locking with the disused launch pad. The sounds sent unadulterated panic raced through his veins.

Cressida sat up in bed before he could wake her, already alert. "What's going on?"

He damned himself for their not returning to the command tower last night. He had no way to gauge who had arrived on Haven, no way to defend themselves should unfriendlies decide to explore the old settlement.

Defense? With what weapons?

He hated having to say his next words, hated the fear that had crept into his voice. "I don't know." He threw off the covers and nearly leaped from the bed. Cressida did the same and they quickly dressed.

He damned himself for not having a weapon.

Lukas inched open the hut's door and peered outside. He could see telltale puffs of steam and coolant rising from the launch pad, but he couldn't see the ship itself. He relaxed a smidgen. That meant it was too small to be a commercial or military vessel.

He felt Cressida's presence behind him, heard her panicked breaths. He reached behind him and gripped her hand. "We're going to make a run for the command tower," he said, keeping his eyes on the immediate area. "I can find out more about our visitors there. As fast as we can go, all right?"

"Yeah."

It wasn't nearly as much fun as it was yesterday, but both of them bolted across the scrubby ground for the command tower. Lukas locked the tower door behind them and they dashed up the stairs, where he quickly connected himself to the comps through wrist port connections.

He scarcely noticed that he didn't feel embarrassed to be doing so in front of Cressida.

Images of the trespassing ship assaulted him. It was small, as he guessed back at her hut, and an older model based on the amount of steam issuing from its braking vents. It was too large to be considered a personal shuttle and too small to haul freight.

Lukas analyzed the ship's specs as they whizzed along in the corner of his vision: the *Raider*, a private passenger transporter based out of Center City on Echo-7, currently registered to a Captain Janek Dalton.

The hairs on the back of his neck prickled at the mention of Echo-7 and Center City.

He was able to grab the *Raider*'s passenger manifest and his heart skipped a couple of beats when he saw the sole name listed. Valenna Merchant, also of Echo-7.

Should he tell Cressida that her sister had come to Haven as some sort of rescue operation?

Nearly every cell in his body screamed not to and to simply tell Cressida to hide until the *Raider* left. He desperately wanted to listen to that notion but knew in his bones that if he didn't tell her Valenna was here, even though she'd washed her hands of her sister, that Cressida would never forgive him. The planet wasn't big enough for two people angry with each other, and he wouldn't be able to bear it if she hated him.

He closed his eyes, wishing the ever-present data readout would stop once in a while, let him truly be alone with his thoughts. Even a few seconds to collect himself would be enough.

"It's Valenna," he said, his voice flat and unrecognizable to his own ears.

Beside him, Cressida sucked in a harsh breath. "What?"

"Your sister hired that ship to come here. She's here now."

"I don't understand," Cressida said softly. There was a wobble to her voice as if she was on the verge of tears. "How did she find me?"

He sidestepped the obvious answer to that question. "What do you want to do?" Lukas couldn't look at her yet, couldn't tear his eyes away from visualizer watching the *Raider*. Its exterior door opened and a ramp unfolded itself on the launch pad. The ship looked far too small for the gigantic space.

"What do you mean? I want to stay with you, Lukas." She curled a hand around one of his arms.

"Do you want to speak to her?" He didn't want Cressida to think she was a prisoner here.

It would rip out his heart, but if she wanted to leave, he wouldn't force her to stay.

He chanced a look at her. The desolation and uncertainty on her face tore at him.

"I don't know," she said. "I've already said my goodbyes to her. I haven't spoken to her in over a year. I couldn't deal with her anymore, and right now ... Lukas, I don't know what to do." Before he could form a response, she shook her head. "No. She does *not* get to interfere with my life anymore." She sniffled and wiped at her eyes. "No, we're staying here."

Two masked figures strode down the *Raider*'s ramp, one a slight dark-haired woman about Cressida's size and the other a giant of a man. He had a field bag slung over his shoulder and he stomped down the ramp and through the carnibo trees with the deliberate, heavy step of a soldier, over the double-thorned rose bushes, and then out of visual range. The smaller woman jogged to keep up with him.

A chill slithered down Lukas's spine. This was a man on a mission, someone already familiar with Haven's terrain. He quickly racked his brain, trying to recall Janek Dalton and coming up empty.

"I lost them," he said and pulled the datalinks from his wrists.

"What do you mean, *you lost them*?"

"They moved out of range of the working visualizers. Your sister and that ship's captain are looking for us," he said. "We're going to go downstairs and I'm going to see if I can find a working weapon, okay?"

The desperation on her face tore at him. "Come on, Lukas. There's nothing here to defend ourselves with."

"Then you'll hide," he said. "I'll try not to come across them, but if I do, I'll tell them you died in that fall and I dumped your body in one of the ponds." At her horrified expression, he added, "They'll believe a cyborg did that, Cressida.

But there was one more tactic they could try. "Unless you want to speak to Valenna, tell her you're all right and ask her to leave."

Cressida paused for a second, considering. Finally, she shook her head. "No," she said. "She has an ulterior motive coming here, I know it." She squeezed his arm. "And we stay together. You won't go out and tell them some bullshit story about my dying in a fall. They can't know you're here, and if you kill them, I'm sure someone will miss that captain."

She was right. "Then we'll stay in here and barricade the door," he said.

"What if they start looking around? They'll find my hut occupied."

"And you won't be there," Lukas said. He felt some of his confidence returning. "Haven is an inhospitable planet."

"They'll assume I accidentally walked into some quicksand or was bitten by something lethal."

"Exactly."

They'd stood around talking for long enough. Lukas grabbed her hand and they quickly descended the stairs. He checked to make sure the heavy front door was bolted shut, then he led her to one of the storerooms on the first floor to look for a weapon.

There wasn't much, he thought as he closed the storeroom door behind them. A couple of antiquated laser rifles, charges long since dead. An ax. He picked it up, hefted its weight. He hoped to the universe he wouldn't have to brandish it, let alone actually use it. Cressida's eyes flickered in concern but she didn't protest.

Maybe they would leave if they didn't find Cressida. He prayed for it.

A few heavy thumps sounded at the exterior door. Cressida gave a small shriek. "Maybe we shouldn't come at them with weapons if they break in," she said, her voice a harsh whisper. "If they come in here, they'll believe me when I say I want to stay here because I want to, not because you're holding me hostage."

He didn't believe that, but he still lowered the ax, leaning it against the wall. "We'll wait here," he whispered. "Hopefully they'll get bored."

There was another succession of heavy muted thumps, followed by a large bang as the exterior door was forced open. Heavy booted feet slammed across the floor.

Despair raced through Lukas. It was foolish for them to have been so optimistic about their chances of being left alone.

He was going to lose Cressida. Because he knew whatever happened today, this Captain Dalton was going to find a way to take her away from him.

He gripped Cressida's hand. "I love you," he said. "Finding you and everything that came after that—this has been the happiest time of my life. The *only* happy time of my life."

"Lukas," she said harshly. "I'm not going anywhere. I'm not leaving you and we're staying on Haven."

The storeroom door was slammed off its hinges to the floor. This time Cressida didn't try to silence her scream at the sight of the two masked figures from the launch pad.

"Here you are, Cressy!" said a sunny female voice.

The male figure nodded his head slightly at Lukas and Cressida. "Lieutenant Best," he said, reaching into his field bag. He dropped something on the floor and a small mushroom cloud of smoke had both of them coughing and choking. Cressida sagged against him and he held on to her, his sensors picking up on her losing consciousness.

As was he.

He tried to will his body to run an antidote, but his cybernetic system didn't respond.

Panic welled up in him as he slid to the floor, Cressida still in his arms.

The last thing he saw before his eyes closed was the huge form of Captain Dalton looming over them.

The unfamiliar rumble of engines eased Lukas awake. He tried to move and found limbs tethered to his seat, and he fought back a wave of nausea.

He was in space, for the first time in years. He didn't have to look out a viewport to know that.

He turned his head to the side and saw Cressida strapped into the seat next to him, still sleeping, although she was untied. There was another, unoccupied pair of seats across from them. "Cressida," he whispered urgently.

She didn't stir.

He looked around the small, dimly-lit cabin. He knew where they were, the only question was where Captain Dalton was taking him and Cressida. She was probably bound for Echo-7, but as for him ...

The captain had known his name and rank. The *Raider's* appearance on Haven hadn't just been for a rescue mission. Dalton was looking for Lukas, too.

Valenna appeared in the cabin doorway, dark circles under her eyes. "You're up," she said. "How's Cressida doing?" She peered at her sister and brushed a lock of dark hair off her forehead. She plunked down in one of the seats across from them.

Lukas sidestepped her question. "Where are you taking us?"

"Oh, I'm taking Cressy home," Valenna said. "Janek said he's collecting a bounty on you."

"There haven't been any bounties posted for me in years." He'd occasionally tapped into the galactic net at great risk to himself to find that out. Admiral Best seemed to have given up on searching for his AWOL son.

Valenna shrugged. "I don't know. I don't really care, either. I just want to get Cressy home."

Lukas narrowed his eyes. "According to Cressida, you two haven't spoken in over a year. She doesn't speak highly of you." A fine sheen of sweat had popped out along Valenna's brow, and the slight tremor of her hands hadn't escaped his notice.

She was in withdrawal.

Valenna seemed unperturbed at that statement. "When your sister goes missing, you start looking for her."

"How the hell did you know she was missing? She cut you off!"

That seemed to spark some of Valenna's ire. "I wanted to get back in touch with her," she said. "I went to her apartment, found it empty, and her neighbor said she hadn't returned from her holidays. Her work said the same thing and they'd terminated her employment."

She'd probably gone to Cressida's looking for more scrip.

"I did some of my own investigating and found out that a passenger wasn't accounted for on the ship she took to that jungle," Valenna continued. "It wasn't hard. I hired Captain Dalton and he agreed to take me here."

"How did you pay him?"

Valenna bristled at that question. "I have money."

The *Raider* lurched forward for a stomach-churning moment, and the sharp whine of the hyperspace engines underneath them made any more conversation impossible. Valenna fell back in her seat, and Lukas saw her mouth the word "Fuck!" at the impact.

Hyperspace gates were always a bitch to get through when it was unexpected. What kind of captain was Dalton, not warning his passengers to brace for the impact?

There was a loud grinding noise, and then quiet was restored as the ship was pulled into the calmness of hyperspace. Cressida stirred.

Valenna stood up on shaky legs. "Cressy!"

Cressida blinked and turned her head to Lukas. "Oh, thank God." Her voice was a croak. "You're all right."

"Cressy!" Valenna waved her hand in Cressida's face. "Remember me?" She held out her arms for a hug.

Cressida stretched her arms and legs. Anger replaced the

relief on her face when she took in the sight of her sister. "What the hell is going on, Valenna?"

Shock suffused Valenna's features. "That's it? 'What the hell is going on'? No thanks for saving your ungrateful ass?"

"No!" Cressida shouted. "What the fuck was that, drugging us?" She glared murder at Valenna, who lowered her arms. "And do *not* start with me about ungrateful asses, Valenna."

"We needed to drug Lieutenant Best," Valenna said as if that made a difference to what she and Dalton had done. "That was the agreement I had with Captain Dalton. We're taking you back to Center City and he's going to deal with the lieutenant. You know he's been AWOL for years, right?"

"No," said Cressida. "You turn this ship around right now and take us back to Haven."

Valenna stared at her incredulously. "You can't be serious!"

"Cressida," said Lukas softly, "It doesn't matter. They know where I was." His gaze fixed on hers. "There's no going back to Haven."

She shook her head. "No. We stay together, Lukas. I'm not leaving you." She reached for his hand and froze. She turned to Valenna. "Why the fuck is he tied up?" She picked at the ties only to find them locked.

"The captain said it was necessary."

Cressida's tone was sharp enough to cut glass. "Untie him."

"I'll have to run that by Dalton, and he's still on the bridge."

Lukas discreetly flexed against the ties. They were strong, but he could probably break them off if he had the chance. He relaxed a little in his seat. "Cressida," he said, "It's okay." He tried to convey that message in the look he sent her way.

She seemed to understand and backed off. She clasped his

hand, and that small touch sent a wave of reassurance through him.

When she spoke again, her voice was calm, level. "I'm not going back to Echo-7," she said. "Wherever Lukas goes, I go with him."

Surprise, then understanding dawned on Valenna. "Oh, my God, Cressy. You're fucking the cyborg?"

Neither of them offered a rejoinder to that, but Lukas clutched her hand a little more tightly.

"Ugh," Valenna added.

"Fuck you," Cressida snapped. "Why did you come looking for me anyway?" She gestured around the passenger cabin with her hand. "How did you pay for this?"

Her reply to that question was just as petulant as the one she gave to Lukas. "I have money."

"No, you don't," Cressida shot back. "You know you're shivering, right? How long has it been since your last darfin hit?"

Valenna looked a little discomfited at those words, but she still answered. "Long enough. I'm fine."

"Valenna," she said. Her words were slow and deliberate. "How. Did. You. Get. The money?"

Her sister avoided eye contact and shifted in her seat before standing up and stalking out of the passenger cabin. "Ungrateful bitch," she said over her shoulder.

"She probably pawned everything she owns and everything in my apartment," Cressida said as soon as Valenna was out of earshot. "Lukas, let's get you out of those restraints." She swayed a little on her feet when she stood up, a residual effect of whatever had been in that smoke bomb, but she easily righted herself.

"They're locked," Lukas said, "But they don't feel very strong."

"To a cyborg," she said.

"To a cyborg, yeah." He flexed his forearms and raised them as much as he could. His left restraint popped first.

"Oh, thank God." Cressida started picking at the right restraint's lock. Between her nimble fingers and Lukas's strength, they were able to make short work of it fairly quickly.

His leg restraints were easier. Once they were torn off, he collected her in his arms and branded her with a kiss. "I love you," she whispered in his ear. "I'm not leaving you. We're in this together, no matter where they take us." Her eyes searched his face. "Do you think we could take over the ship?"

He desperately wanted to say yes, to offer her that reassurance, but he could never lie to her. "I don't think so," he said gently. "We don't have the ship specs, nor do we know where we are. There aren't any ports here for me to connect to. We need to speak with the captain and see if he can be reasoned with."

"Well, I can't say I didn't try to restrain you."

The deep male voice startled both of them. Janek Dalton stood in the cabin doorway, mask off and a laser pistol in hand. Its charge glowed yellow, set to stun. That was a minor relief.

"Are you going to try to kill me?" Dalton asked.

"No."

Dalton looked surprised. "So you're going to cooperate?"

"You have my complete cooperation provided Cressida isn't harmed," Lukas said.

"Don't worry about that," Dalton said. "While Ms. Merchant's priority was finding her sister, mine is turning you in for a decent bounty. The military posted it years ago."

And as far as Lukas could tell, they'd given up trying to find him nearly as long ago. "I'm not so sure they want me back."

"I'm sure you can imagine how delighted I was when I ran a scan when we landed on Haven and picked up your biosign,"

Dalton said. "Good bounty hunters are always on the lookout for fugitives."

Lukas stilled. What kind of tech did this ship have, anyway? And the bounty hunter himself, for that matter? "What am I worth to the military?" he asked. "The last time I checked it was around twenty-five thousand scrip." The amount was far less than he thought it would be, considering the millions that had been poured into building him, but it wasn't something to sneeze at, either. It was more than a year's salary for most of the denizens of the Zone.

Dalton nodded. "It hasn't been updated in years. I was surprised about that." He sat down opposite him and Cressida and leaned back in his seat. "You had a lethal reputation in the military."

He didn't want Cressida to know the details of what he'd had to do during his time in the service. "I know."

"I was expecting a bigger fight from you, to be honest." Dalton steepled his fingers and waited for a response.

"With what?" Lukas said. "Haven's been abandoned for years. Almost everything useful was taken when the installation was decommissioned, including weapons." He took a deep breath. "I wasn't going to put Cressida in a position where she could get hurt."

She shifted on his lap a little and leaned her head against his shoulder. He didn't need the sensors in his hands and gloves to feel her unease and distrust of the man.

"Captain, I went AWOL because I was tired of killing things," Lukas said. "I didn't want to just be a robot anymore. I still feel that way."

Dalton shrugged. "It makes no difference to me. I spent time in the military, I know what it's like. But I have to earn a living somehow."

Once again, Lukas was someone else's commodity, a chunk of metal and wires in a man's body to be ordered around. The familiar rage at not being considered human rose in him, but he refused to act on it. If Cressida hadn't been clinging to him, he wouldn't have hesitated to stun Dalton himself and commandeer the ship back to … well, not Haven. That wasn't a safe place anymore. He'd dump Dalton and Valenna at the nearest sketchy spaceport that didn't ask any identifying questions and take the *Raider* to parts unknown.

Anywhere, he thought. He'd go anywhere but back to the Zone, as long as Cressida was with him.

"You couldn't find a more savory way to earn a living, Dalton?" Lukas asked him.

"You've been out of the Zone far too long, Lieutenant."

Not that Lukas had had any idea of how the average person survived in the Zone even when he was a boy, but he didn't interrupt Dalton.

"I can either transport passengers to wherever they want to go, no questions asked, and pick up fugitives on the side," Dalton said, "Or I can work eighteen hours a day in a petrik mine until an explosion kills me. It wasn't a hard choice to make after I was discharged."

"Who did you serve with?"

"Two Hundred and Twelfth Battalion, long before your time," Dalton said. "I was honorably discharged thirteen years ago." He grinned. "Are you looking in all your directories, trying to remember me? You wouldn't. We were on opposite sides of the Zone."

Bastard. Lukas glared at him.

Cressida spoke up. "How did Valenna pay you to get me?"

"She was looking for a ride to Haven and some darfin."

"Yeah, I figured she'd be looking for that."

"I was happy to provide both and she was able to pay."

Cressida shuddered against Lukas. "She's probably getting high right now," she said into his shoulder.

Dalton piped up again. "That sounds about right." He

stood up. "I'm not going to try to restrain you again," he said to Lukas. "We both know you're going to fight back."

He wouldn't if it meant keeping Cressida safe, but he didn't let that on.

"I'm locking the cabin," Dalton said. He crossed the short distance to the cabin doorway. "Poke around all you want, you won't be getting out of here. I'll see you when we arrive in the Zone."

Dalton slid the door closed and engaged the locks.

CHAPTER 10

DESPITE HER BEST efforts to remain awake, Cressida still caught a few snatches of sleep, curled up in Lukas's arms. She had no idea how much time had elapsed since they were taken from Haven, nor was she entirely certain where they were exactly headed. There was any number of cheap, unsecured spaceports around Echo-7 where an unscrupulous bounty hunter could leave them.

And what about Lukas? Where was he going? Cressida's knowledge of the military, as she'd told Lukas so long ago, was extremely limited. She had no idea where most of their bases were located. The Zone was a big system.

Because if the *Raider* intended to leave her and Valenna at a spaceport in Center City, she would fight back tooth and nail. She wasn't leaving Lukas.

The rumble and vibrations of the ship's engines increased beneath their feet, the telltale sign of breaking atmosphere. "Do we fight?" she asked Lukas.

His gaze was flinty, and for the first time since he hauled her out of that double-thorned rose bush, she saw the soldier that still lived in him. Not the brutal cyborg he'd alluded to being at one point, but the man he'd always been through his training, his cybernetic surgeries, through wars. Lukas was determined, and, she guessed, he had a plan.

"Not yet," he said.

Some of her confidence wavered a little. "Really?"

He tilted her chin to face him. "I told Dalton I'm going to cooperate," he said. "We both are. You're going to go back to Echo-7 with Valenna and I'm going to do something I've been putting off for years."

"But you'll be court-martialed!" Or worse. Cressida had heard only the barest of rumors about the military's treatment of soldiers prior to being marooned, some of them being confirmed by Lukas.

She felt her heart being pulled out of her body as the *Raider* succumbed to the gravity of wherever they were landing.

"Cressida," Lukas said. His voice was soft but firm. "You have to trust me on this. We're going to get out of this mess. I promise."

"But how...?"

"Please," he said. "I'm still a soldier. I'm still a cyborg. I have some capabilities that will help us out." He brushed his lips against hers, and tears welled up in her eyes. "I'll find you. No matter where you are, I'll find you, sooner rather than later."

Cressida's mind raced, all the possible blocks to their escape—*his* escape—tumbling through it. "Where do you think you'll go?"

"There are a few possibilities," he said. "None of which you'll be able to access as a civilian. Don't come after me, Cressida. You'll get yourself killed. The Zone military has a 'shoot first, ask questions later' policy when it comes to their bases and settlements, civilians included."

His words did nothing to reassure her, but she still nodded in agreement.

"I mean it," he said. "Promise me you won't do something stupid if we're separated."

Rescuing him from whatever hellhole he might find himself thrown into didn't count as stupid in her book, but she knew he would disagree. So she nodded.

"This is still my world," he said. "I do know how to navigate it, even if I don't want to."

He'd been away from that world for years, but Cressida refrained from pointing that out. How much could the military have changed, anyway?

A grinding noise belowdecks, followed by a loud hydraulic whine as the *Raider*'s landing struts extended, told them that they were nearly at their destination. There was a series of clanks as the struts engaged with the spaceport's locking clamps, and a few moments later the engines went silent.

The passenger cabin door opened, and Dalton appeared in the doorway, weapon trained on them. It didn't escape Cressida's notice that the charge indicator glowed red, set to kill. "Get up, Cressida," he said.

It took a few seconds for his words to register, and Lukas's hands pushing her off his lap for her stand up. She ignored the pins and needles running through her legs as she faced Dalton.

"This is where you and Valenna leave," Dalton said. "She's awake but she's polished off her darfin supply. She says she can find more here."

"Where are we?"

"Echo-7," the captain said, exasperation in his voice. "Where else would I take you? You're at Eben Spaceport, so right on the route home back to Center City."

She looked back at Lukas. "Where are you taking him?"

Lukas gave her a warning look but didn't say anything.

"That's none of your concern," Dalton said. "But you need to get the hell off my ship before I shoot him."

Lukas had survived being shot before, but she didn't know

if he could make it through a laser strike in such close quarters, to say nothing of the pain involved. "I'm standing up," Lukas said, his hands against the armrests. "I'm not going to do anything but say goodbye to Cressida."

Dalton nodded but didn't lower his weapon.

"I suppose it's too much to ask for some privacy," Lukas said.

"Yes. I've paid for twelve minutes of dock space here. Hurry the fuck up."

Lukas kissed Cressida with an intensity that left her weak in the knees. "Remember what I said," he whispered into her ear. "Don't do anything stupid and don't try to find me. I'll get us out of this, and I'll find you."

"I live in the twenty-fourth apartment block at Center City Estates," she said. "Unit 1632." Her mind worked rapidly. "At least I did before. I don't know…"

"It's okay," he replied. "I'll find you, no matter what."

"Can you hurry this up?" Dalton said, sounding bored.

"I love you," Cressida said.

"I love you, too." His dark eyes fastened on hers. "And I'll see you soon."

Cressida had never been to Eben Spaceport, but she'd heard about it. Anyone who lived in Center City had. Due to its lack of enforced security and cheap, per-minute docking fees, it was a hub for unsavory characters and activity. She had no doubt that Valenna was happy to be dropped off here, to make it easier to pick up more darfin.

Valenna stumbled to Cressida's purposeful strides, occasionally trying to grab at Cressida's backpack for balance. That was the only bright spot in this whole miserable situation: at some point after Dalton smoke-bombed her and

Lukas, he or Valenna had thought to look around the settlement for Cressida's stuff. They'd probably looked in the hut first, she thought. She couldn't remember if they'd closed the door in their mad dash back to the control tower. She'd checked her backpack immediately after Dalton kicked them off the *Raider* and found her thincomp, holographer, wallet, and a military-issue shirt inside.

She would be able to access her bank account, at least. And when she had the opportunity, she could connect to the galactic net and see if she could find out the likeliest places Lukas would be held.

"Slow down," Valenna mumbled. She dug her hand into Cressida's arm, nails digging in through her shirt.

"No," Cressida said, and kept up her pace. Valenna didn't relinquish her grip.

"Your apartment's still there, you know."

"I don't care," Cressida said. "I don't care about that apartment or what I left behind. Or my job." She stopped and Valenna nearly lurched into her. Cressida met Valenna's red-rimmed, watery eyes. "Why did you come after me? How did you get the money to pay Dalton?"

"You're my sister," Valenna said, voice high in frustration. "That's what sisters do, right?"

"No, Valenna." Cressida struggled to keep her voice level, not wanting to draw attention to themselves. "Sisters don't drift in an out of each other's lives for the sole purpose of shaking them down for money. Sisters don't *steal* from each other. Don't you remember breaking into my apartment, waving around a black market stunner when you robbed me?" She felt the burn of tears behind her eyes and blinked. "I should've let the police file charges." Her voice increased a few decibels of its own volition. "They don't force them away from the love of their lives, Valenna!"

Valenna looked at her, incredulous. "Look, I'm sorry about the break-in."

"*That's* what you're taking away from all this?" Cressida quickly walked away, following the directions for the nearest exit. She could get back to Center City proper on the next shuttle. According to signs posted around the spaceport, they departed every fifteen minutes.

Valenna hurried to keep up. "Cressy, he's just a cyborg, you know that right?" she called behind her. "Dalton said the military doesn't even make them like him anymore, and he ran away besides. He said he needs to be reprogrammed."

A new, horrifying idea took shape in Cressida's mind.

Could the military do that? Would Admiral Best order Lukas's mind, his feelings and thoughts, obliterated? Finally turn him into the mindless, ever-obedient killing machine he'd been so reluctant to be?

"I need Dalton's contact information," Cressida said urgently.

Valenna scowled. "I found him through ..." She fumbled for words. "A friend."

A dealer, she really meant. How many times had Cressida heard her sister talk about "friends"?

"I don't know how to contact him," Valenna said. "And Cressy, that lieutenant is basically a robot. You can tell your friends you got to fuck a robot if you want because that's pretty out there, but you need to move on."

Never, including the time Valenna robbed her and threatened her with a weapon, had Cressida wanted to bodily destroy her sister.

And should she really be surprised that an amoral bounty hunter like Jarek Dalton would associate with darfin dealers?

She bit back a cry of frustration and forced herself to remember Lukas's last words to her.

Don't do anything stupid. I will find you.

She could still look, with or without Dalton. The Zone was a big place, but not so big to lose their military's first cyborg success story.

Valenna swayed on her feet, waiting for a response. Cressida nearly walked away and left her at the spaceport, never to see her again, but she had one more question that needed to be answered. "How did you get the scrip to pay Dalton?"

Valenna actually looked a little scared at that.

"Did you steal what's left of my belongings?" Cressida pressed. "Contact my bank and tell them to transfer my funds over to you?"

"No, they said they couldn't do that."

Of course not, Cressida recalled. She hadn't filed a will naming heirs. Per Zone estate laws, any assets she had upon her death were to be absorbed by the state instead. She hated that the small amount of money she'd managed to sock away might already be in the government coffers, contributing to the military and Lukas's fate. But at least Valenna hadn't managed to get her paws on it.

"They said not enough time had passed," Valenna added.

That meant Cressida could still access to her bank account, which would make her life a little easier. It didn't ease the sting of knowing, once again, that Valenna Merchant was a manipulative, thieving narcissist, but it would help.

"Did you sell one of your organs?"

Valenna bit her lip and looked down at the dirty tiled floor. "I moved some stuff for my dealer," Valenna mumbled.

Drug smuggling. *Of course.*

Cressida dug through her backpack and removed her palm-sized scrip chip from her wallet. She could pick up a strong connection to the galactic net at Eben Spaceport and was relieved to find out that the chip still worked. When she pressed her thumb into the small disk, green numbers glowed back on its tiny screen. Her bank balance was significantly higher than it was supposed to be.

What the hell?

That was something else that needed to be investigated, and she wanted to do it right away. She took a final look at Valenna.

She felt no sympathy for her sister, no desire to see her ever again.

Without another word, she strode through the spaceport's corridors, breaking into a run over Valenna's protests, headed for the nearest exit and the shuttle that would take her back to Center City.

Cressida managed to lose Valenna in her dash for the shuttle. Her sister had made a half-hearted attempt to keep up but finally yelled, "Fine, Cressy, fuck you, too!" before she reached the shuttle.

Cressida picked a seat near the door, close to the pilot, and pulled out her thincomp. Connected to the galactic net for the first time in weeks, her messages tab lit up. She checked through them—mostly from her employer, demanding to know where she was, a couple of concerned notes from colleagues, and receipts for her apartment's automatic rent, water, and air payments. She breathed a tiny sigh of relief. At least she still had a home to go to, even if Valenna had raided it again. Cressida refused to believe that she hadn't.

There was one more message, this one from MacQuarrie Galactic Holdings. The name was vaguely familiar, but it wasn't until she opened it that she realized what it was.

Dear Ms. Merchant,

We regret that you did not have an exemplary experience aboard the Gryphon. *Per our customer service agent's conversation with your next-of-kin, Valenna Merchant, we have refunded your round-trip ticket cost and will provide a future third-class ticket aboard one of our ships to the destination of your choice, subject to terms and conditions outlined below.*

We apologize for the inconvenience.

The words sent shockwaves through Cressida, and she barely noticed the shuttle taking flight toward Center City.

Valenna, she thought. Valenna had come around for whatever reason, found out she was missing and asked around to her neighbors as to where she might be. Then she got in touch with MacQuarrie Galactic, the only line Cressida or anyone living in the Center City apartment blocks could afford. That might account for why Cressida was reported missing and no one bothered to look for her; Valenna wouldn't have wanted to involve the police in any way, not with the record she had.

Not for the first time, Cressida regretted not filing charges against her sister for that break-in.

She looked back down at the message. *We apologize for the inconvenience...*

Yeah, being marooned on an abandoned military settlement was merely an inconvenience to them. The company had accurately guessed that she wouldn't have the means to sue. Not that she would. Her being left behind meant she met Lukas.

He had made her promise she wouldn't do anything stupid, and she wouldn't. Because tracking down and saving him didn't fall under that category.

CHAPTER 11

TRUE TO HIS WORD, Lukas cooperated with Dalton after Cressida was thrown off the *Raider*. He paced the short length of the passenger cabin, trying to stave off the ache in his heart at her loss while he tried to figure out where he was and how he was going to escape. It wasn't until the heavy air engines engaged that he was forced to take his seat again as the ship fought the gravity of whatever planet he was being taken to.

The list of possible places was fairly long. The Zone's government had maintained any number of installations and black sites around their space, both planetary and manmade stations. All Dalton had to do, at least as far as Lukas knew, was leave him anywhere with a military presence and collect the twenty-five thousand scrip Admiral Best had placed on his head.

I'm only worth twenty-five thousand after all that training and surgery. Beads of sweat popped up along his brow as his body fought against the pull of gravity. Now that Cressida was off the *Raider*, Dalton clearly didn't see fit to engage any comfort controls in Lukas's holding space.

Not me, he reminded himself. *The tech in my body.* No one had ever cared about Lukas Best, the man, just what he could do loaded with sensors and machinery.

Until he rescued Cressida.

He had meant every word when he said he would find her. He would go along with whatever Janek Dalton and the military wanted from him, and then escape again. Cyborgs had a way of integrating with technology to make it work to their advantage. Dalton knew that, based on the lack of available dataports in the passenger cabin.

Thirty-two minutes passed between the ship's rough heavy air landing and Dalton unlocking the cabin door according to his data readout. The captain again held his weapon in hand, the charge still glowing a deadly red. "Get up," he ordered.

Lukas again held up his hands and waited for instructions.

"We're going to disembark the *Raider*," Dalton said. "We've landed on Garshan."

Lukas didn't try to hide the surprise that he knew flitted across his face.

Garshan was the last place he'd expected to be taken to.

It took him a few seconds to find his voice. "There isn't an installation here." At least there hadn't been before he went AWOL. Nor was there a black site, but of course all of that could have changed in his years away.

"We're going to disembark the *Raider* together," Dalton said. "You're going to walk ahead of me, and I'm going to keep my gun at your back. Do you understand?"

"I've lost track of the number of times I told you I'd cooperate with you."

"I doubt very much that a cyborg with an eidetic memory would forget how many times he told me that," Dalton said.

Well, the bounty hunter wasn't technically wrong.

"I focused on the development of my human side on Haven," Lukas said.

"But you're still a cyborg and still worth that bounty,"

Dalton replied. He gestured to the cabin doorway with his pistol. "Let's get moving."

Lukas slid past the captain and stopped once he was clear of the doorway, not moving again until he felt the weapon's barrel between his shoulder blades. If Dalton made that shot it would kill him.

"Walk," Dalton ordered. "Straight ahead, then turn right at the end of the corridor."

Lukas did so, noting the *Raider*'s shopworn interior. Its walls were dented metal devoid of any personal touches, with darkened alert sirens near the ceilings. The deck was made of a pitted metal grating, the occasional remnants of dingy, colorless carpeting visible from where it had been carelessly stripped out. They passed a couple of closed doors, including one labeled BRIDGE. That one had three locks on it.

He could smell fresh air as they kept on walking, and he had to blink once they reached the *Raider*'s exterior ramp. Bright sunlight and the heavy, cloying smell of berrylace trees assaulted his senses, nearly triggering his gag reflex.

Nowhere else in the Zone did berrylace trees grow. They were too expensive to maintain, too temperamental for any climate other than a warm one year-round to thrive. They were a status symbol on Garshan, and he knew before his eyes adjusted to the sunlight that he was on the property with the largest collection of them on the planet. "You brought me to my father's estate?"

Dalton made a non-committal noise in response.

"I'm going to raise my hands to shade my eyes," Lukas said. "I haven't seen sunlight like this in a long time and it'll take a couple of minutes for them to adjust." He'd actually liked Haven's perpetual overcast sky in retrospect.

"I don't care," said the captain.

The *Raider* was docked at the Best family estate's personal launch pad, still as meticulously maintained as it was the last time Lukas was here. Half a kilometer away the Bests' ancestral home beckoned, a sprawling monstrosity whose imported whitestone exterior sparkled in the sun. Like the berrylace trees, whitestone was a delicate material and cost far too much money to keep in good repair, so naturally, it was revered by his tasteless ancestors.

And his father. He mustn't forget that.

An unmanned anti-grav flitter waited at the launch pad, a two-seater that had been part of Lukas's family fleet since before he could remember. He didn't need Dalton to prod at his back with his pistol to walk down the ramp to the flitter, but the bounty hunter did it anyway.

He got in first and slid over to make room for Dalton, lowering his hand as his eyes adjusted to the sunlight. Dalton activated the vehicle with his palm print, and the small vehicle took off toward the house.

"I suppose we're expected," Lukas said.

Dalton shot him an irritated look. "Yeah."

The flitter stopped in front of the house's main entrance, partially obscured by more berrylace trees. A long-buried memory resurfaced at the sight of them and their bright blue-green leaves: Lukas's mother, now passed on for seventeen years, had loathed them and continually argued with the admiral to remove them.

She had come from an old, well-decorated military family as well and Lukas suspected that his parents' marriage was an arranged match. They hadn't liked each other that much anyway, nor did either of them particularly care for their young son. Eria Best had been devoted to two things: religion by way of the Great Faith of Stars and horticulture.

Cressida had liked horticulture, too. At least she'd enjoyed puttering around in Haven's hydroponics.

Don't think about Cressida right now or what she could be

going through. You will have a chance to save her again very soon.

Eria hated the smell of those trees, hated the expense that went toward keeping the damn things alive. Lukas remembered her hopping into one of the flitters—maybe even the one that brought him and Dalton to the house—and intentionally uprooting one of the trees, remembered the hours of fighting that small act of rebellion produced. Lukas's father had had the tree re-planted, and that was the end of that argument.

Dalton pointed at the door. "Get up and walk over there."

"You know, I could have figured that out myself," Lukas said, but he complied.

An uncharacteristic nervousness churned in his stomach as they walked to the door, which opened with a near-silent hiss at their approach.

A round-shouldered old man waited, his remaining silver hair neatly clipped against his scalp, a walking stick in hand.

It took Lukas a few seconds to realize that the man waiting for them was Admiral Best.

How could someone age twenty years in less than six?

"Admiral!" called out Dalton from behind him. "Look what I have for you!"

Lukas and Dalton stepped inside, the interior unchanged since the last time he visited. Despite his advanced age, Admiral Best still had a powerful aura about him, one of a man who was used to being obeyed. For all of his faults, the admiral hadn't been a vain man and clearly hadn't had any cosmetic work done. He looked every day of his seventy-plus years, and then some.

He and the admiral paused, staring at each other. Not for the first time, Lukas itched to clock him one in the jaw, his age and physical condition be damned.

Admiral Best spoke first. "That will be all, Captain Dalton," he said. Even his voice sounded weaker.

"My funds?" said Dalton.

"The bounty was transferred to your account as soon as the *Raider* broke atmosphere," Admiral Best said. "You're dismissed. The flitter will take you back to the launch pad."

Lukas looked at the bounty hunter, clearly surprised at the lack of drama unfolding in front of him. *Sorry to disappoint you*, he thought.

But Lukas was surprised as well, but he couldn't say which element of the scene before him was the most discomfiting: being brought back to his father's house rather than a military installation for interrogation and torture, or his father's health. Why would the old man use a *walking stick* when he had every medical advantage at his beck and call?

Dalton didn't move, but he holstered his weapon. "Are you sure?"

The admiral's tone brooked no argument. "Leave."

The bounty hunter looked at both of them one last time before walking out of the house, the door hissing closed behind him.

Lukas barely noticed that, and judging from the eye contact the admiral kept with him, his father hadn't noticed either.

A few heartbeats passed as they stared each other down.

"You're back," Admiral Best finally said.

"Not by choice."

"I imagine not," the admiral replied. "Come with me. I'm sure you have questions you want me to answer." He turned around and shuffled along the deep pile of the plum-colored carpet beneath their feet, but Lukas didn't move.

"Follow me, Lukas," the admiral said. He paused, then added, "I promise I'm not going to shoot you for desertion."

Cressida's apartment had been ransacked, but nothing appeared to have been taken.

She smoothed out the rumpled covers on the bed—had Valenna taken a nap in her apartment?—and connected her thincomp to the galactic net, running as many search strings as she could think of, trying to get a bead on where Lukas might have been taken.

There was nothing in the news about an AWOL cyborg soldier being taken into custody again, nothing that gave her an indication of where a military deserter might be held.

She searched for bounty hunters as well, hoping to pick up some more information about Janek Dalton. She found nothing; black market bounty hunters didn't seem to advertise their services on the publicly-accessible galactic net.

Lukas had told her not to do anything stupid. Charging off through Zone space, forcing her way into military bases in her hunt for him, would definitely qualify as stupid. She'd probably be shot on sight at the first base she landed at.

Tears welled up in her eyes, and for the first time since she returned to Echo-7, she let them fall.

What the hell was she supposed to do?

The logical course of action would be to get in touch with the education department, explain what happened, and make herself available for a new job. But where keeping herself stuck in a cubicle had once been an annoyance she had to endure, pure terror at the thought of being cooped up in one now made her want to curl up in a ball and cry. More than she wanted to now.

She could sit on her MacQuarrie Galactic settlement for a little while, try and get herself back together until Lukas came or she figured a way to track him down, whichever came first.

Cressida had to believe that. She would lose her mind if she didn't hold on to the hope she would see him again.

"Follow me."

Despite his obvious frailty, Admiral Best's voice still brooked no argument. Not that Lukas would have obeyed him had the order been anything more to walk to another part of the house.

Lukas walked alongside his father, who moved surprisingly quickly for someone dependent on a walking stick. His clothes were gray and navy-blue civilian trousers and sweater, insulation against the house's freezing-cold climate control. But the admiral's back was ramrod-stiff when Lukas walked alongside him, his gaze straight ahead. Even if Lukas hadn't known the admiral he would have guessed the man was military.

The door to the downstairs study opened silently at their approach and lights turned on. "Sit," the admiral said, pointing to a chair in front of an enormous antique desk. The drapes had been pulled tightly shut against the sunlight, just as they always had been, and behind the desk the same massive star chart of the Zone sparkled, delineating every planet and station in the system. Lukas fought the urge to walk behind the desk and find Echo-7.

Nothing had changed in his absence, except his father's appearance. And possibly his father's role in the military. Lukas could count on one hand the number of times he'd seen his father out of uniform in his life.

"Drink?" asked the admiral, opening a liquor cabinet that matched the desk.

"No."

"Suit yourself." Admiral Best removed a bottle of whiskey

and poured a generous amount in one of the heavy crystal glasses Lukas remembered from childhood. His parents had liked to throw them at each other during fights. He wondered idly how many was left of the original set, or if the admiral had had them recreated in a hard-goods replicator.

The admiral took a seat behind his desk, and Lukas sat down in the chair he'd indicated. They stared at each other for a moment, then the admiral took a healthy pull from his whiskey. He was the first to speak.

"It wasn't my intention that you ever be brought back to the Zone from Haven," he said.

Lukas's breathing stilled for a few seconds. Four of them, according to his data readout. "You knew I was there?"

"You did an admirable job orchestrating your escape and it took about seven months for me to figure out exactly where you took off to, but yes, I knew." He took another, smaller swallow and set the half-filled glass on the desktop.

Why didn't you come back for me? he nearly asked, but stopped himself in time. He waited for the admiral to continue.

"I ordered the Fleet to stop their search for you once I learned where you went," the admiral said. "I kept the bounty on you for appearance's sake, but no one was seriously searching for a cyborg with the abilities you have for such a pittance. No one wanted you to kill them. Then the issues with the Brava System started up again and we had other things to worry about."

"Why did you leave me alone?" Lukas asked.

"Because you had good reason to go AWOL. I see that now." The admiral took another drink, then stood up and went back to the liquor cabinet. "Are you sure you don't want one?"

"Very."

"All right." The admiral poured another drink and secured

the bottle back in the cabinet. Lukas thought it might be easier if he just brought the bottle back to the desk, but didn't suggest it.

"We monitored life forms on different uninhabited planets and installations around the system," Admiral Best said. "You did very well at hiding yourself on Haven, but we did figure out you were there eventually. I assume you destroyed the shuttle you stole to get there?"

He may as well answer that question. "I stripped out the hardware components and comm array and sank them piece-by-piece in the quicksand pits. It took a few days."

"And you stole Captain Purcell's personal shuttle rather than a military craft," the admiral recalled. "Not using a traceable military shuttle gave you a good head start. Although I must say Purcell was quite angry about the theft."

"Purcell used to test out new weapons set to stun on me. I don't regret stealing his shuttle."

"He was dishonorably discharged four years ago, for what it's worth. It wasn't just the stunning incidents."

Of course, it wasn't. Lukas wasn't, and never had been, a person to the military.

"Under my orders, Haven was listed as a forbidden territory," Admiral Best said. "Off limits to all military, commercial, and personal craft, although I see a few ships ignored that instruction over the years."

"Their landings on Haven was for repair-related purposes," Lukas said.

"I know."

"Why did Janek Dalton come after me?"

Admiral Best swallowed another mouthful of whiskey. "Dalton is one of the most amoral bounty hunters in the Zone. Certainly the worst I've dealt with. He wasn't afraid of a cyborg soldier."

"He smoke-bombed me out of my home."

"I didn't intend for that to happen. I didn't intend for anyone to ever contact you."

Lukas found himself leaning forward, wanting more answers. "How did he know where to find me?"

"I understand he was contacted by the sister of a woman who was marooned with you on Haven," Admiral Best said. "The sister was quite insistent that she be found, dead or alive, so she could either collect on her worldly possessions or get money out of her. Frankly, from Dalton's description, the sister sounded like a piece of work."

"She is," said Lukas.

"Dalton figured out the likeliest place the woman—"

"Cressida," Lukas said.

"Yes, Cressida. He figured out she was probably on Haven, then noticed there were no-travel orders on the planet. It appears he used a biosign scanner to look for her, then noticed two people living there."

"How?" Lukas demanded. "I kept tabs on any ships or shuttles nearby and didn't pick up anything on my scanners."

"The remaining hardware left on Haven is over ten years old," the admiral said. "Your own tech is nearly as old. Dalton also had access to advanced black market tech. Lukas, it was only a matter of time before someone noticed you were there. I'm actually surprised this didn't happen earlier."

"And even though you unofficially quarantined Haven, you still permitted Dalton to go ahead and kidnap me and Cressida?"

It was the admiral's turn to look surprised when Lukas worded their predicament that way. "Was I supposed to have stopped him? Let him babble to every other bottom-feeding bounty hunter and criminal in the Zone that an AWOL cyborg was on the loose?" It was Admiral Best's turn to lean forward, elbows on the desktop. "Let you be sold into some black market lab where you could be pulled apart and examined?" Before Lukas could respond, he said, "No, I didn't want that. The safest course of action was to allow you to be brought back to me in one piece and pay out the bounty."

Shock suffused Lukas at those statements, and once again he found himself speechless. When he could form the words, he said, "I've already been pulled apart and examined. Repeatedly. On your orders."

"I know, and I didn't want you to go through that again." The admiral locked his gaze on Lukas's. "I was wrong to do that, and I take full responsibility for all of it. The whole cyborg project was an inhumane failure."

Lukas gripped the chair's armrests, trying not to let his feelings show.

Was the admiral *apologizing*?

No, not quite. But he'd just admitted wrongdoing for the first time in Lukas's memory

Regret flashed over his face before he continued. "You were never a son to me. Nor to your mother, truth be told. You were always a project in need of improvement. An achievement I could be proud of."

"You were never proud of me." Lukas hated that the words were petulant, but he still wanted to say them.

"No, I wasn't. My expectations were unrealistic and cruel. I didn't understand that until I found out where you took off to, and I realized you needed to be left alone. Or at least far away from me and the Zone."

Lukas didn't want to hear any justifications for what his father had done, only needing to know what his plans were. "What happens now?" he asked.

"What do you mean?" The admiral raised his glass and drained it.

"Am I to be returned to military custody for a court-martial?"

"No. I'll arrange your formal discharge." The admiral set down the glass on the desktop, the noise loud in the study.

"I'm discharged." Lukas's words were flat, disbelieving.

"Yes. Honorably so." He stood up and put the glass in the wall-mounted recycler. "You deserve that. I'm not going to ask for, nor do I expect, exoneration from you, Lukas."

"You wouldn't receive it anyway," he said. "Just because you owed me an apology doesn't mean I owe you forgiveness."

"Of course not. But I can send you on your way and hope you'll find some level of contentment that you couldn't find in the Zone."

I can send you on your way.

Lukas's heart nearly stopped as he registered the words. "You're letting me go?" With an honorable discharge, no less.

"Yes," the admiral replied simply. "You can go back to Haven, for all the universe cares. It's still a quarantined planet and always will be. You have my word that no one will come looking for you under my orders."

Lukas rose to his feet, uncharacteristically unsteady from the shock. "You aren't going to shoot me in the back before I leave your property?"

"No. I'm going to stay here." He rapped the desktop with his knuckles.

"I need a shuttle."

"Take one from the launch site." Curiosity still flitted across the old man's face. "May I ask where you're going?"

Lukas didn't detect any maliciousness from his father, no ill intent. He still hesitated before answering. "Echo-7. Center City."

"That's a dirty planet."

"I promised to meet someone there."

"This Cressida? Don't be coy with me, Lukas."

Lukas had never been coy. That had been all Cressida. Memories of her in the hydroponics tub, chasing her across the anti-grav gym, raced through his mind. "Yes. She's worried about my being reprogrammed or tortured."

Admiral Best's expression softened just a little. He cleared his throat before speaking. "Whatever she means to you ... I hope there's some happiness there for you."

"There will be." Already he was thinking about how long it would take to get to Echo-7 and find her. He hoped like hell she hadn't gone off looking for him yet.

He and his father stared at one another for a few seconds before Lukas looked away. "I suppose this is good-bye."

The admiral nodded. "Yes."

Without another word, Lukas turned around and walked away.

CHAPTER 12

CRESSIDA'S THINCOMP dinged another incoming message. Irritated, she checked her inbox and scanned the contents. She'd been put on a waitlist for a new apartment in her block. She would have to wait at least three months before a new unit was made available. Three more months where Valenna knew her address. *Fabulous.*

Maybe she should just look for at another apartment block altogether. Lukas had said, after all, that he would find her no matter what.

Had he escaped yet?

She'd been scanning every news broadcast she could find, desperate to see if his capture had been made public, and came up empty every time.

She printed the holos she'd taken of him and the pair of them together, and they now graced her apartment walls, the images providing little relief. If anything, they made her miss him more.

Don't do anything stupid, she reminded herself again.

She spent yesterday in vidconference with MacQuarrie Galactic, both to point out the absurdity of their settlement offer to someone they couldn't get in touch with and to tell them how she managed to sneak off the *Gryphon*. She'd been deliberately vague in her description of the flight attendant she'd bribed to get off the ship, but the customer service agent she spoke to assured her that a full investigation would be undertaken.

Cressida couldn't be angry with him. She'd ended up meeting Lukas thanks to him. But she was level-headed enough to know that had Lukas not been living on Haven she would have died.

She couldn't bring herself to care about the attendant's fate after that investigation was concluded. She still hurt too much, couldn't be bothered over her own selfishness.

A knock rapped against her apartment door.

She looked at it, alarmed. Hardly daring to hope it wasn't a neighbor or, God forbid, her sister.

No, Valenna would just break in.

Cressida jumped from her bed and swung open the door, and nearly burst into tears when she saw who waited there.

Lukas stood before her, his clothes civilian-issue dark green and black, a new backpack slung over his shoulder.

They stared at each other for what felt like an eternity, Cressida not trusting her eyes.

"You're here," she said, her voice a whisper.

He tossed his backpack inside her apartment, then took a cautious step toward her. She grabbed his hands and pulled him inside, then closed the door.

"I'm here," he said. "I told you I'd come for you."

"You escaped?" she said. She looked around her apartment. She could pack up her essentials and be ready to run with him in just a few minutes.

"No," he said. "I was discharged. Honorably so."

That ... was not the answer she was expecting. "How?"

"My father let me go," Lukas said. "He knew I was on Haven and he ordered it quarantined." He cleared his throat.

"It's a long story and I'll tell you, but he regretted doing what he did to me. His leaving me alone and then discharging me was his way of apologizing." His mouth quirked up in a smile. "I'm a free man, Cressida."

Before she could form a reply, he kissed her with an intensity that sucked the breath from her lungs. She let him guide her through the small apartment until the backs of her legs hit the edge of the bed, and he gently pushed her down on the mattress. He slid in next to her on the narrow space.

They needed a bigger bed. A bigger apartment. Assuming they would stay in Center City. Cressida didn't care, as long as she was with him.

He rolled on to his side and looped an arm around her to keep her on the bed. "We can do whatever we want," he said.

She nodded, unable to speak through the lump in her throat.

"No one's going to bother us again," he said. "The admiral guaranteed that."

It took a few heartbeats to find her voice. "I was thinking about coming after you," she said. "But ..."

"I told you not to do anything stupid," he reminded her.

"I know. Do you know how hard it was to trust you when you said you'd come back for me?"

"I know how hard it was being apart from you," he said. "And we're not going to be separated again. I love you, Cressida."

"I love you, too." She threaded her fingers through his, noting his gloves were gone. She looked at him quizzically.

"I don't need them," he said. "I'm just a man now, Cressida." She must have made an alarmed face, because he quickly added, "No one's touched me. But I'm just going to be living a regular life here, with you. Or wherever you want to go." Uncertainty flitted across his face. "If you'll still have me."

"Of course!" She let go of his hands to wrap him in a hug,

made awkward by the small bed. "Damn it, we'll have to find a bigger place. I'm already on the waitlist to move."

"We can do whatever we want," Lukas said.

"Finally." Cressida pressed a hungry kiss to his mouth, felt his body respond in kind beneath her. "As long as we're together."

ABOUT THE AUTHOR

Jessica Marting is a sci-fi and paranormal romance author, art enthusiast (not quite an artist, despite all that time in art school), an avid reader, and makeup collector. She lives in Toronto.

Sign up for her newsletter at jessicamarting.com/newsletter for pre-order alerts, sales, freebies, and more.

ALSO BY JESSICA MARTING

Magic & Mechanicals

Wolf's Lady

Sea Change

Bound in Blood

Dragon's Keep

Zone Cyborgs

Haven

Paradise

Oasis

Safe Harbor

Sanctuary

Refuge

The Commons

Supernova

Celestial Chaos

Standalone Novels & Novellas

Spindle's End

Trade Secrets

Neon Vice

Dead Ringer

Escape From Europa 10

Castaways

Demon's Favor